# Gone Daddy Blues

## Books by Jane Tesh

### The Grace Street Mysteries
*Stolen Hearts*
*Mixed Signals*
*Now you See It*
*Just You Wait*
*Baby, Take a Bow*
*Death by Dragonfly*

### The Madeline Maclin Mysteries
*A Case of Imagination*
*A Hard Bargain*
*A Little Learning*
*A Bad Reputation*
*Evil Turns*

# Gone Daddy Blues

## A Grace Street Mystery

### Jane Tesh

Savvy Press

First Edition 2020

Library of Congress Control Number: 2020935851

ISBN: 9781939113467    Trade Paperback
ISBN: 9781939113474    Kindle

Savvy Press
479 Beattie Hollow Rd
Salem NY 12865
www.savvypress.com
info@savvypress.com

Cover design: François Thisdale

Printed in the United States of America

To Ellen Larson, editor and friend, who showed me how to write a mystery novel, who taught me many useful computer skills, and who made sure I didn't implode.
I would not have a writing career without your guidance, and since that was all I ever wanted and all that defines me, the least I can do is dedicate a book to you. Maybe two.

# Acknowledgements

When your ship is sinking, it is amazing to discover how many of your friends have lifeboats.

My thanks to Mary Flinn for sharing her publishing experience, to long time writing buddies John Shivers and Laura Wharton for their advice and encouragement, to Linda Parks for proofreading the final manuscript, to Ellen Larson for her excellent writing and publishing skills, and to François Thisdale, whose beautiful covers capture exactly what I have in mind when I envision 302 Grace.

# Chapter One

### *"Gone Daddy Blues"*

S ome wise man, Confucius, maybe, once said: Into each life, some blond must fall. In my case, three blonds. Kary you know about, and as for the others, well, I'll let the story unfold. Or maybe I should say unravel.

I was sitting in my office that cold Friday November morning, feeling sorry for myself. You'd think I'd be filled with the pride of success. A recent client had been extremely pleased when I'd found his glass dragonfly, so pleased that on top of my regular fee, he paid me ten thousand dollars. Ten thousand extra dollars to help my struggling detective agency, located in a downstairs parlor in Camden's boarding house at 302 Grace Street, which was also my home. Back in the summer, I cleared our friend Rufus Jackson of murder charges and found his baby girl. Plus Kary and I had moved our relationship a giant step forward into the physical realm. So hurray for me.

It wasn't that easy.

The perks of being a private investigator are many and varied. My latest case involved finding a deadbeat dad whose gambling addiction had ruined his family. I'd hoped for a happier settlement. I couldn't stop thinking about his little girls, their sad eyes and shaky sobs. I'd had several of these gone daddy cases over the past few months and the result was always the same. Broken promises. Broken families. I'm good at finding things, I really am, but I was beginning to think some things were better off not found. I wanted to do something meaningful.

So when the first blond arrived, I was not in the mood for any sort of investigation. She was a skinny girl, all hard angles, hair tied back in a scraggly ponytail, eyes like gray flint. With her faded jeans, ugly plaid flannel shirt, scuffed boots, and large leather pocketbook bumping on her bony hip, she looked like she'd been riding the trail for the Pony Express. She came into my office and dug into the pocket of her jeans. She brought out a crumpled piece of paper. She consulted the paper and scowled.

"You David Randall?"

"Yes."

She reached into her saddlebag and brought out a wad of bills. She plunked them onto my desk. "I want you to find my dad. He owes me."

I unfolded the bills and smoothed them out, giving myself time to think. "Please have a seat." She perched on the edge of the chair I have for clients. I started with the usual questions. "What's your father's name?"

"Arliss Padgett. I'm Doreen Padgett." She watched me count the bills. Forty-five dollars. "If that ain't enough, I can get more, but Buddy told me you'd help out. He said you had a knack for finding things. I last seen Padgett at the Springdale Trailer Park on Old Dobbins Road just south of Tecknilabs. Lot eighty-seven."

She waited, apparently satisfied she'd given me enough information. "When was this, Miss Padgett?"

"A week ago Friday. He was supposed to pay Mama her alimony so's we could pay the rent, but I haven't seen hide nor hair of that lousy bastard. I done told Mama he run off, but she don't believe me."

"So you'd like me to find him and the alimony money."

"Hell, yeah. That's why I'm here. He's done this one too many times to me and Mama, and I ain't gonna stand for it. I want his sorry ass in jail."

From overhead, I could hear a steady hammering. Camden was on the roof, replacing shingles that had blown off during last week's rainstorm. Doreen Padgett's gaze was as hard as the nails he was pounding and as deep as the headache I was getting. Another deadbeat dad. Great.

"Any particular reason why you chose this agency?" I'm always curious why people choose the Randall Detective Agency. I'd solved a few high-profile cases in town, but I still hadn't gained a wide reputation.

"Buddy said you'd do it, even though I'm just turned eighteen. He's the one what give me your name."

Eighteen. Good lord. I must have looked as startled as I felt, because Miss Padgett made a face that suggested this was the least of my worries.

"Listen, mister, that ain't gonna be a problem." She looked me up and down like a pro. "You're a good-looking man, but you ain't my type."

I'd been cut before, but this was deep. "I didn't mean—"

"Yes, you did." She smirked and tossed her dirty blond ponytail. "But that's okay. You guys are all alike." The smirk faded, replaced with her intense flinty stare. "I'm hiring you because Buddy said you'd do it, and who else is gonna take me seriously? Besides, that's all the money I got till next week. Buddy said you'd help me out. He said you were good at this."

Just what I needed, an unsolicited testimonial from Buddy. Ever since I'd let him check out a suspect for me, which mainly involved hanging around the Crow Bar, his favorite hangout, he thought he was an unofficial partner in the Randall Detective Agency.

I looked at Doreen Padgett's hard little face and made a decision. "Sorry, Miss Padgett, but I'm no longer in the deadbeat dad business."

"Buddy said you'd do it," she repeated, as if these were the magic words. "What's the matter? Scared you can't find him?"

She actually said "skeert," if that's how you spell it.

"I imagine I can find him. The question is do you really want him found?"

She looked at me as if I'd suggested something improper. "Didn't I just say so? Ain't you been listening?"

"I think you need to try someone else."

As she looked down at her little pile of money, I felt a surge of guilt. I hadn't meant to imply that her offer was unacceptable. She looked back at me, her flint gray eyes anxious. For the first time, she looked eighteen. "I know it ain't much, but believe me, I'd be grateful if you found Padgett, I really would. Come on, mister. I don't know what else to do."

*Daddy, really.*

The sudden message from Lindsey was a shove from the Other Side. I must have looked startled because Doreen said, "What? Did I say something wrong?"

"No, not at all." How to explain I often heard from my little daughter, even though she died in a car accident years ago? Usually I received her messages in dreams, but she was pulling out all the cosmic stops today. What if she'd gone to someone for help and was turned down just because he was in a snit?

*You need to help Doreen.*

*I heard you loud and clear, baby.* I picked up the stack of bills. "Well, then, you're in luck, Miss Padgett. One last deadbeat dad."

Her anxious look changed to a smile of relief. "That's what Buddy said."

Maybe I should have it engraved on my business cards. "Do you have a picture of your dad?"

"Yeah, Buddy said you might need one." She reached into the saddlebag and handed me a well-worn driver's license. "This old license we found back of a drawer."

The photo on the license was creased and faded, but I could make out the charming features of Arliss Padgett's thin face, squinty eyes, and lank dark hair.

"Thanks," I said. "Is there a number where I can reach you?"

She gave me her phone number and swung the strap of her giant pocketbook back onto her shoulder. I walked her out to the foyer, and she peered into our living room, a large open area we call the island because of the group of comfortable chairs and sofa parked in the middle of a worn multicolored carpet. The morning sun gave the room a nice glow, and Cindy, one of our house cats, lazily batted at a ball of yarn that had spilled from Kary's basket by the coffee table.

"That looks nice," Doreen said. "This whole house yours?"

"No, it belongs to a friend of mine. I rent a bedroom upstairs and this office."

At this point, Camden came around the corner from the kitchen, a glass of iced tea in one hand and a Pop Tart in the other. Since he was about Doreen's size, and had on jeans and a sweatshirt, he looked about her age. I introduced them.

"Camden, this is my newest client, Doreen Padgett. Doreen, this is Camden."

"Hi," he said. "Nice to meet you."

She gulped, a faint pink blush coloring her thin cheeks. Apparently, short sloppy men with untidy pale hair were her type. She took a few moments to recover. I could see her pulling herself out of the depths of Camden's blue eyes, and he wasn't even using a power gaze.

"Hi, yourself," she said.

With his Pop-Tart, Camden indicated the roof. "I'm almost through with the right hand side, Randall."

"Great. I'm tired of all that hammering."

"Would you care for some tea, Miss Padgett?"

Doreen looked as if he'd offered her champagne. She shook her head. "I gotta go. I'll be late for work at the Quik-Fry. Know where that is? Just a few streets over from here."

"I stop by there all the time. I love their cheeseburgers."

Doreen's expression suggested she'd gladly get him all he wanted. "We fry them. That's why they're so good."

"Hence the name," I said. I got a dagger look from Doreen.

She readjusted the strap of her pocketbook more securely on her shoulder. "I gotta go. Nice meeting you, Camden."

I escorted her to the door and told her I'd let her know the minute I had any news. Then I went back to the kitchen where Camden was spooning extra sugar into his already too-sweet tea.

"Isn't it nice to know you can still excite teenagers?" I said.

He took a bite of Pop-Tart. "You keep forgetting I'm a married man."

I took the peanut butter and a box of crackers out of the cabinet. I figured I'd need sustenance before attempting to find Arliss

Padgett. "Heard anything from the missus?"

"She's having a great time. Keeping that vortex spinning."

"It will, too, if it knows what's good for it." Camden's wife, Ellin, was off on a sacred mission: live reports from New Mexico for the Psychic Service Network's fifth anniversary show. The PSN was still alive and kicking. Apparently, I was the only one who saw through all the nonsense.

I made some peanut butter crackers and hunted in the fridge for a cola. "Did she say when she'd be home?"

"Don't worry. I'll give you plenty of warning."

"You could always just move me out of the way."

Camden had always had a great deal of psychic ability, but back in the spring, he suddenly developed a talent for telekinesis. We decided the outbreak had been due to wedding anxiety. He hoped it would go away once he and Ellin tied the knot, but it continued to pop up. He'd been able to halt runaway cars as well as killer dogs, two tricks that had come in handy during a previous case.

Although he wasn't sure what his powers were going to do next, Camden was looking forward to fatherhood. He'd seen three children in his future. Actually, he'd seen them in Ellin's. He couldn't see his own future. Two girls and a boy, he said, all psychic. I didn't care if they were psychic or not. I just hoped to God they inherited their father's disposition and not their mother's.

Camden sat down at the counter that separated the kitchen from the dining area. "Did that fellow come by about the room?"

"Nope. Never showed."

"Damn. We need another tenant."

Our long time tenants, Rufus and Angie, had found a house on River Street, two streets over from Grace. Camden had made shelves for the garage and was fixing the kitchen cabinets. They'd moved out last week. Vermillion, the faded flower child who'd rented another room, found her soul mate in Wally the plumber and moved in with him. Kit, our latest boarder, found success with his rock band, Runaway Snakes, and was on the road. He'd sent us several videos of himself wailing on the guitar, python Slim over his shoulders, and Slim's big brother, Jim, coiled around the drums. That left me and Kary on the second floor, and Camden and Ellin on the third. Our one paying tenant was blond number two, Lottie Lee McAllister, a nutty little friend of Kary's, who thought she was a mystery writer. She was also on the second floor and fortunately spent most of her time in her room.

I brought my snack and joined Camden at the counter. I took a sip of cola. "What about that lady from church?"

"She's decided to move in with her daughter." He ran his hand through his disheveled hair. "Hope you didn't want anything for Christmas."

"Something'll turn up. We always manage. Isn't Ellin getting a bonus for this vortex gig?"

"The Psychic Service paid for her plane ticket and hotel, that's all."

"Aren't you getting paid for a couple of weddings?"

He nodded. "And for the tenor solo in 'Messiah.'"

During the holiday season, Camden's vocal cords were even more in demand. "Did you decide about that opera, the one about the three kings?"

"I can't do that one. Not enough time, not with the cantata at church and the choral society concerts."

"They were going to pay you for the opera."

"I'd already promised the other groups. Ellie and I had a real good argument about that before she left."

"I know." It was hard not to hear their conversations, especially because Ellin had a voice that could penetrate steel. Ellin had never liked the idea of living at 302 Grace with the rest of us peasants. Her on-going complaint involved house hunting, which Camden didn't want to do. She seemed to think he purposely stayed at a low-paying job and didn't take money for singing so he couldn't afford to move. She was right.

Camden rubbed his forehead. "And that car crash is still with me."

Last week, there had been a serious head-on collision on I-40. To try and settle the argument about which driver caused the crash, the ambulance driver had brought a piece of the damaged van for Camden to hold, hoping he could see the truth. He'd seen the truth, along with mangled body parts, spurting blood, and an eye where it wasn't supposed to be.

"Isn't that over?" I asked. "Didn't they decide the other guy was at fault?"

"Yes, but I'm still having reruns."

"Are you seeing the same crash, or different ones?"

"The same one."

"Maybe that's significant."

He gazed into his tea glass as if it held the answers. "Maybe it's just freaky. I swear I am never touching anything for anybody again."

"What can I say? You gotta deal with it."

He swung his power gaze my way. "Speaking of dealing with it, what's this about finding Doreen's dad? Lindsey had to give you a push."

Not only does he know what's on my mind, he also hears from Lindsey. "You two don't need to gang up on me."

"You've always said you want to find things for people. You can't give up, Randall."

"I'm not giving up. Shouldn't take me too long to find her dear old dad. Which reminds me—"

He cut me off. "No, thanks." Even if he hadn't been psychic, he knew what I was going to say. We'd been over this territory many times.

I'd located Camden's mother. She'd given him up for adoption when he was three days old. She told me she didn't want to see him, but had surprised us by coming to his wedding. The two of them were getting to know each other. The only thing she could tell us about his father was that his name was Martin and he looked like Camden. Camden said he doesn't want him found, but I knew damn well he was lying. Besides wanting to punch his dad in the eye for abandoning him and his mother, he wanted to know all about the weird power he thought he inherited from this man, what it was going to do next, and how to handle it. Finding Martin had become a challenge for me.

"Okay," I said. "Thought you might like to know which planet to call home."

This earned me a dark look. I knew he harbored a secret fear that because of his considerable psychic ability, he might be an alien, or possibly the result of some UFO inspired pregnancy.

"Don't you have someone else to find?" he asked.

Before I could answer, the doorbell rang. I went to the front door and opened it. "Flush the marijuana," I called to Camden. "It's the police."

Jordan Finley, one of Parkland's finest, shouldered his way in. "Very funny."

"What's up? I paid all those speeding tickets."

He gave a snort. "As if that heap of yours could get past thirty-five." He removed his cap and his brush-cut black hair stood at attention. "Cam, how long are you going to let this freeloader stay here?"

"A little longer," Camden said. "Come in, have a seat. You want a drink? A snack?"

"A doughnut?" I asked.

"You're such a comedian, Randall. No wonder people flock to your agency." He folded his tall square figure to sit down on the green corduroy sofa. "Actually, I need a favor."

I parked myself in the blue armchair. "Be still my heart."

"Not from you." He scowled and turned his attention to Camden. "Cam, I know you don't like to do this sort of thing, but we're in a real bind here. Three women have been found murdered, and from the look of things there may be a serial killer on the loose. We've got zip. The chief remembered how helpful you were finding that lost jogger last year, and before that, when the McElroy boy was taken, how you helped us find the kidnappers. He asked me to ask you, unofficially, of course. There're a lot of people downtown who don't hold with clairvoyance."

"How can I help?" Camden asked.

"I'd like for you to see if you can get anything off one of the victim's blouses. It's out in the car."

Camden hesitated. He'd just sworn off touching things, and I knew holding a murder victim's clothing was potentially a nuclear blast to the brain. "I don't know about that."

"It would really help us out."

Camden glanced at me. I gave him a serious roll of the eyes.

"Let me think about it," he said.

"We don't have a lot of time. This guy's likely to strike again at any moment."

He took a deep breath. "Okay."

When Jordan went to get the blouse, I said, "You don't have to do this. Think about it. A serial killer. A real weirdo. Murder victims. You'll be a wreck."

"Maybe not. Maybe it won't be so bad this time."

Jordan came back with a paper bag. He took out a torn yellow blouse and handed it to Camden.

As he touched it, he winced. "He's cutting off her hair."

Jordan shot me a quick look. "Yes, all the victims had their hair cut off." He looked back at Camden. "What else, Cam?"

Camden's expression was puzzled. "Why is he cutting off their hair?"

"We don't know. Do you see anything else?"

His voice drifted to another tone. "Long hair. Long and soft, like Margaret's. She never cut it. It was always so long and soft. She never turned around. She never looked at me. All I ever saw of her was that long soft hair."

Now Jordan's glance was alarmed. He started to say something, but I shook my head. I'd been through this territory before.

"Who are you?" I asked Camden. "What's your name?"

He gazed way beyond us. "Long hair. So beautiful."

"Yes, it is. What are you doing with it?"

His eyes shifted, wary. "Making something."

Great. A quilt? A wall hanging? "I'd love to see it. Where are you?"

Abruptly, the moment was over. Camden shook his head to clear it and shuddered. "God, this guy is creepy," he said in his normal voice. "I couldn't see his face, but I felt his extreme caution, his long fingers. He's obsessed with women's hair. Blond hair."

"All the victims have been blond," Jordan said.

Camden continued to touch the blouse. "I thought I might get something else. That's all. Sorry."

"Don't apologize," Jordan said. "At least we have a name to start with. If I bring you some more things, would you try again?"

"Sure. There's nothing painful, just a really strange feeling, like being in a fog."

"A fog of hair," I said. "Sounded like you were channeling him for a minute."

Camden smoothed the blouse. "I could feel his fingers stroking long hair." He shuddered again. "Even after he cut it off, he kept playing with it."

"Jordan," I said, "I want to thank you for bringing this lovely case into our home."

He put the blouse back in the bag. "What's it to you? You're not getting involved. Thanks, Cam. You going to be okay?"

"Yeah, sure."

Jordan reached into his jacket pocket. "I need a cigarette." He made a slight movement with his head, gesturing me to follow. Outside, he leaned against his patrol car and tapped a cigarette out of the pack. "I hadn't seen him do that. On the other cases, he just pointed out the location."

"You got the multimedia version today."

"Is he all right? He looked, I don't know—"

"Like ten miles of bad road?" One of Rufus' sayings.

"Yeah. Ten miles of bad road on the moon." Jordan started to light his cigarette and paused. "He's not going to turn into this killer, is he? I mean, will this creep take over his mind? Good God, I never meant for anything like that to happen."

"I don't know," I said. "I guess we'll find out."

Jordan lit his cigarette and took a deep pull. "This whole psychic thing is beyond me. You ever wonder about that stuff?"

Since the whole psychic thing was not beyond my realm of experience, this was an easy question to answer. "Every now and then."

"Well, you keep out of it."

"Don't worry," I said. "I have a really hot case going."

Jordan raised an eyebrow. "Let me guess. Another deadbeat dad."

"Number four hundred and thirty-two."

He blew out a long stream of smoke. "Another idiot on the loose."

I'd met Jordan's father, an older, tougher, white-haired version of Jordan, a retired cop and good husband, who'd brought Jordan and his two brothers up to be sensible, dependable human beings. My own father, despite a roving eye for the ladies, had always been there for me. Like me, Jordan had trouble understanding the pathetic losers who deserted their families, duds who called themselves dads.

Jordan got into his car. "Keep an eye on Cam, Randall. If he starts acting really weird, he's off this case."

"Depends on how you define 'really weird.'"

He couldn't leave without giving me his standard warning. "And you stay out of this case."

A warning I always managed to ignore.

# Chapter Two

## *"Do Right Daddy Blues"*

I went back to the island. Camden had gotten himself a can of Coke and another Pop-Tart. He gave me a wry smile. "So much for swearing off clairvoyance."

I sat back down in the blue armchair. "If you can help Jordan catch this nut, then it's a good thing."

"It wasn't as intense as the crash, thank goodness, but I never know." He plopped down on the sofa. "Every time I get a vision, I don't know if it's going to be useful, or take my head off."

"You're squishing your Coke can."

He looked down at the twisted can. "I get so frustrated when I can't control it. I wish to hell I'd never been born this way."

"Okay, I'll see about getting you some more drugs."

"No, thanks." The pills that stopped the visions stopped everything else, too. He wasn't going to take a chance like that again.

A voice sang out, "Oh, good, here you are!"

Camden and I looked at each other and said, "Damn." We'd not been paying attention, and now we were caught. Lottie Lee McAllister trotted down the stairs and into the island, carrying one of her ever-present spiral notebooks. Her round little face was alight, her round little body quivering with excitement. She looked harmless, a plump retired schoolteacher with short graying blond hair and guileless blue eyes behind overlarge glasses, but in the time she'd been in the house we'd learned to avoid her if at all possible.

"I finally finished this chapter of *Desperate Hours* and I'd love to have your input. I think I figured out where to put the sailboat scene, you know, where Randolph swims out to rescue Preston, just like you did, David, when Camden was drowning."

Someday, I'd have to take Kary aside and remind her not to tell people about my adventures, especially people like Lottie Lee McAllister.

Lottie squeezed herself onto the sofa beside Camden and turned a page in her notebook. "It goes right here, just after the jewelry heist. The spies from Bulgaria have kidnapped the princess, and they're heading for the border. When Preston went after them, he was captured, and now they've tossed him overboard."

Preston, the useless sidekick, "adorably fair and youthful, with eyes you could drown in," was short, blond, and blue-eyed, like Camden. I fared a little better. Davidson Randolph, her hero, was tall, dark, and handsome, like me. Actually, the description she'd written was "dark and arrogant, like the prince of some rich un-known country, always looking for other lands to conquer." I'd suggested she add "and other women." Ellin was her model for Helena Bell, "a strikingly attractive career woman." The striking part was right. Kary was Carrie Invers, a beautiful blond model, "like a princess in a fairy tale." Maybe it wouldn't have been so bad if Lottie could write, but she put the ack in hack. Her plots made no sense, her dialogue was trite, and her prose kept the engines humming at the cliché factory.

Camden took the notebook, his eyes widening as he read. I waited to see what sort of creative compliment he'd manage.

Lottie leaned against his shoulder to point to a certain passage. "Did you get to the part about the tiger yet? I thought it would be so exotic for the villain to have a tiger on his yacht."

"It's different. I think I like *The Raging Rapids* better, though."

"Do you? Do you really? But Preston's hardly in that one. He's recovering from Yellow Fever."

Which is why Camden was probably able to get through *The Raging Rapids* without heaving.

Lottie was anxious for feedback. "Let David have a look."

Camden gladly passed me the notebook. I took it and read.

"'Davidson Randolph knew he had only a few moments before his friend would be lost to him forever beneath the cold dark waves of the pitiless ocean. Summoning all his resources, he made one final lunge toward the last place wherein he had viewed his faithful companion.'" I made a slight drowning "woof" under my breath and Camden choked on a laugh. "'With one final lunge, he grasped into the black water, and his seeking fingers connected with the unresisting arm of Preston.' Just the arm, Lottie? Hope the rest of Preston was attached."

"Oh, my, yes."

"Skip to the part about the tiger," Camden said.

I turned a few pages until I came upon another passage. "'The evil Basil Farthing could only have one animal as wild and cruel as he to share the confines of his elaborate floating palace. That was a Bengay Tiger, the most fearsome of beasts.'" Okay, well, I was done now. "Lottie, don't you mean a Bengal tiger?"

She took the pages back. "Isn't that what I said?"

"You have Bengay, which is great for those aches and pains, but doesn't really run about the jungle being wild and cruel."

She waved her hand back and forth, shooing the elusive Bengay tiger away. "I can fix that later. What do you think about Basil?"

"I never missed an episode of 'Fawlty Towers.'"

She blinked at me a few times and then laughed. "Oh, the comedy show. That's right, the main character's name was Basil. He was a lot sillier than my Basil, though."

"Basil sounds like an interesting character," Camden said. "Maybe if you told a little more about his back-story, your readers would understand his motives."

She gave a little gasp. "That would explain why his eyesight is so bad."

"His eyesight?"

"I don't know why I didn't remember this! He wears nothing but opals, and you know opals can dim your eyes or even cause you to go blind. He's furious about this, but he doesn't understand. You know the ancient Chinese believed that opals were alive."

Camden was as baffled as I was by this line of reasoning, but he smiled encouragingly. "Well, if you want to go in that direction, he could be looking for a cure and doesn't care who he steps on to get it."

"Then I could change the title to *The Opal's Curse!*" She patted his knee. "That's a splendid idea! That's why I love living in this house. Creativity just oozes from its every pore!" She hopped up. "I've got to write all this down before I forget it!" She paused, concerned. "Now, where did I leave my other notebook?"

"Weren't you working out on the porch yesterday?" Camden asked.

"Oh, yes. The weather was very nice out there yesterday. I'll bet that's where it is."

Camden waited until she'd gone out to the porch before putting his face down in the sofa cushions to muffle his laughter.

"Good lord," I said. "To think she's one of Kary's friends."

He surfaced. "You can't blame this one on me."

"I know. It's astounding. And the sad thing is, she'll probably sell one of her dreadful books and make a million dollars."

"Then you and I can play Randolph and Preston in the big budget summer movie blockbuster."

"Sounds like fun, faithful companion." I heaved myself out of the blue armchair. "Okay, I've put it off long enough. Time to round up Arliss Padgett."

***

I had gotten into my white '67 Plymouth Fury with every intention of doing just that when Lottie, who'd been sitting in one of the porch rocking chairs and scribbling furiously in her notebook, hurried down the front steps and tapped on my window. She gestured for me to roll it down

"David, would you do me a huge favor and give me a ride to the gas station? I left my car there this morning, and they've just called to say it's ready."

"Sure," I said. "Hop in."

She trotted around to the passenger's side, got in, and hooked her seat belt. "Thank you so much. Everyone else is at work, and I don't have a bit of change for a taxi."

I started the car and pulled out on Grace Street. "No need to call a taxi."

She smoothed the Fury's dashboard. "Such a wonderful old car! You know, all detectives have some distinctive automobile, like a Firebird or a Viper."

"You can't be a detective without one."

For a moment, she took me seriously, and then she chuckled. "Oh, I see what you're saying. Do you think Davidson Randolph would have a Terracotta?"

My mind searched through the makes of cars until I found a likely choice. "Do you mean a Tesstarosa?"

"Isn't that what I said?"

"That would be perfect for Davidson." I turned onto Food Row. "Which gas station?"

"The Exxon on Parkview. Is there some reason Cam doesn't drive? I find that odd. Most men love cars, don't they?"

"He likes cars, he just chooses not to drive them. He says there are too many things to think about."

"It's a fascinating character trait. I think Preston will be the same way, only his reason is because he was in a tragic accident years ago, a tragic accident that killed his parents. Maybe he was driving! Now he's so overwhelmed with grief, he can't bear to get behind the wheel of a car."

"Not even a spiffy new Terracotta?"

"Of course, there'll be a point in the story when he has to drive in order to save himself and Davidson from the villain. The hero always has to face his worst fear."

Lottie rattled on as I drove towards Parkview. My worst fear was that her car wouldn't be fixed, and I'd have to drive her all the way back home. When she paused for breath, I said, "Kary said you were looking for a house. How's that coming along?"

"Everything I've looked at has been so expensive. I'm really going to have to sell one of my books soon in order to afford anything, even the rent for Cam. I can't tell you how many story ideas I've gotten from living there, and when Ellin has the baby, they'll be even more." She took off her glasses and cleaned them on the hem of her sweater. "What about you, David? Are you house-hunting, or are you planning to stay permanently?"

"I'm staying on for a while, Lottie. Camden might need some help learning how to change a diaper."

"Oh, my goodness." She pointed to a line of little specialty shops on the right. "Do you mind if we pull in here? I almost forgot. I've got to get something for Cam's birthday."

"It's not until February."

"I know, but if I don't get it now while I'm thinking about it, I'll forget."

That I could easily believe. I swung into the parking lot. "What did you have in mind?"

"The other day, Ellin said something about how ratty his bathrobe looked, so I thought he might like a new one."

Camden wouldn't like a new one, but it would please Ellin, and I'm all for that. I found a parking spot and turned off the motor. Lottie started out and then looked at me.

"Aren't you coming?"

"What for?"

"To help me pick it out. You know what he likes."

"Just get a plain blue one."

"Come help me," she said. "I want it to be perfect."

"How many plain blue bathrobes can there be?" I sighed and got out. If she went by herself, it would probably take her all day.

We went into a shop called Paradise Baths. I'll bet there were fifty different blue bathrobes: dark blue, light blue, blue striped, blue clouds, blue sheep. Lottie's eyes were rolling. I finally convinced her Camden would not like a blue robe with deer all over it. She bought the plain dark blue one and then decided she wanted matching slippers. It didn't do any good to explain that Camden went barefoot year round. Slippers had to be purchased.

I gave up and wandered the rest of the shop until she was finished. Paradise Baths was having a sale. Signs everywhere proclaimed: Second Item Sale! Two For One! Buy One, Get One Free! Of course, this sale didn't extend to bathrobes, or I could've had a blue robe with my choice of animal. I didn't see anything I thought Kary might like. She already had a bathrobe, a soft white terrycloth bathrobe that was a size too big and always slipped off one perfect shoulder when she sat down to eat breakfast.

It was these new memories, happy memories that kept me going, that and the fact I could still see Lindsey in dreams. Safe and content in her celestial playground, she was willing and able to help solve my cases. This along with Camden's psychic insight made me wonder if I should rename the Randall Detective Agency the Heavenly Intervention Agency or Spirits R Us.

*Daddy.*

I stopped right in the middle of the aisle, causing the woman behind me to bump into me. I apologized and moved over. Had I heard Lindsey's voice?

*You need to help that girl.*

Definitely heard her that time. *What girl?* I thought. *Do you mean Doreen? I'm going to help her.*

Lottie bustled up carrying two large packages and effectively shutting off any more communication. "I'm ready to go, David."

I gave myself a mental shake. We went back to the car. She put the packages in the Fury's trunk and slid into the passenger's seat.

"What were you thinking about in there?" Lottie asked. "You looked miles away."

"One of my cases."

Her eyes lit up. "Which one? Can you talk about it?"

"No."

She nodded as if she'd expected this short answer. "Then let me tell you about Davidson Randolph's latest caper."

Ordinarily, I would have run away screaming, but right now, Davidson Randolph's latest caper was the ideal thing to keep my mind occupied. Fortunately, we got to the gas station before Davidson could really screw himself up. Lottie's car was ready. She thanked me again and transferred her packages to the trunk of her beige Accord.

She closed the trunk. "You know, David, if you ever need help with your cases, I'm available. I've read tons of mysteries and true crime books. I could be an excellent resource."

She looked so earnest, I had to smile. "Thanks, Lottie."

"I know I'm a bit of a scatterbrain, but I'd love to be useful. I think of everyone at Grace Street as my family. Anything I can do, you just ask."

Everyone at Grace Street was my family, too. She waited for a reply, so I said, "Well, thanks for the offer. I'll keep that in mind."

I drove until I found a place to pull over and get settled. I waited, hoping Lindsey would reconnect. During a previous case, Camden and I had freed a ghost trapped in a mirror, and not only had Delores thanked me with hidden jewels, she told her ghost pals what a fine detective I was and started sending them to me for help. Then she did something unexpected. She found a way to let Lindsey be the conduit for those spirits in need.

I'd given up trying to explain it. I accepted it. Why not? I was grateful I could still be with Lindsey. If she wanted me to help Doreen, then I'd better get to work.

# Chapter Three

### *"Oh Daddy Blues"*

First, I went hunting for Buddy. For drinks, I prefer Talley's downtown, or the Elms out by the shopping center, but the Crow Bar's a nice place, not too fancy, not too dark. A large screen TV takes up one wall, usually tuned to ESPN. Stools with black leather cushions line the bar; sturdy wooden chairs surround small tables. At the end of the bar, a ceramic statue of a black crow wearing a top hat and hoisting a mug greets the patrons. From the looks of the crow's feathers and glazed eyes, he'd hoisted enough beer to keep him warm all winter. No flying south for this bird.

Buddy was at the bar, talking with the bartender, a skinny fellow named Delbert. Put a few black feathers on Delbert, and you'd have another crow. He was hunched and irritable, with lank black hair and a crooked nose. But he remembered everybody's name and let the regulars run up considerable tabs. Rufus said he even enjoyed a good brawl every now and then, to add a little color to the place.

"Randall," he greeted.

"Give me whatever Buddy's having." I took the seat next to Buddy. This involved moving the stool to avoid the overflow of Buddy's butt. He's only slightly smaller than Rufus, say, your basic stegosaurus, with the same fashion sense and a deceptively dull expression. "About Doreen Padgett."

Buddy pushed up the brim of his dirty cap. The slogan on this cap said, "PETA: People Eating Tasty Animals." "You mean she hired you? You gonna take the case?"

"What am I supposed to do after such a glowing recommendation? What's the story with Arliss?"

"No account white trash."

Delbert set a beer in front of me. I thanked him and put some bills on the bar. "That narrows it down."

"You talking about Arliss Padgett?" Delbert said. "A pathetic excuse for a human being."

"So where do I find the particular rock he's under?"

"Westville, just over the Virginia border," he said. "That's one of his hideouts. Or you might try any flea market."

"Flea market?"

"He steals stuff and sells it at flea markets. Hell, I've seen him steal stuff *at* flea markets, then turn around and sell it again."

My last trip to a flea market had been years ago, when I was tracking down a stolen Hank Aaron baseball card. It was like stumbling through the worst trash heap America had to offer. I'd never seen so much useless crap in my life. And the people looked like they'd been sleeping in barrels.

"Great," I said. "Any chance he'll have the rent money?"

"Probably not," Buddy said. "That little Doreen works hard to keep her and her mom in groceries. I help them out whenever I can, but if that worthless father of hers would act right, she wouldn't have to struggle so hard."

I took a drink and set the glass on the bar. "Okay, let's say I find him and he pays this month's alimony. What happens after that? Doreen wants him in jail, but she won't get any money that way."

"I don't know. Best thing to do is find her a new father."

"You volunteering?"

He chuckled. "I got kids. Lots of kids. Some I don't even know about."

I checked my watch. I still had a number of stops on my list. "How about keeping an eye out for him?"

Buddy took a swig of beer. "I been looking for him. Can't find him. That's why I told Doreen to hire you."

"Thanks. I look forward to rooting through the flea markets

of Virginia."

He grinned and gave me a wink. "Might find you a treasure."

"Is he living in Virginia?"

"Nah, just roams around."

"Where exactly have you looked for him?"

Buddy let out a resounding burp and patted his chest. "Down at the junkyard, Meechum's bar, the pool hall down on Emerald. Usual places."

"Anywhere else in town?"

"You might check with Janice. She's always chasing him away from her place."

"Anybody he hangs out with?"

"Nah, old Arliss is a loner. When you meet him, you'll know why."

Delbert worked his way down the bar and paused in front of me. "You working on that serial murder case?"

"Not directly. Why?"

"Just asking. It's got some of the patrons spooked, that's all."

I looked around at the clientele. "I didn't know you catered to too many women, Delbert."

"These guys got wives and sisters, ain't they? They don't like the idea of some nut giving the cops the slip."

"Jordan stopped by and let Camden hold one of the victim's blouses."

"Oh, yeah? He see anything?"

"Something that might help Jordan's investigation. We'll have to wait and see." Delbert shook his head. "Damn. What's wrong with people?" Someone called for a refill, and he moved back up the bar.

Buddy frowned. "Thought Cam wasn't gonna do that kind of thing anymore."

"He owes Jordan."

"The way I see it, Jordan owes him. You gonna help out?"

"Eventually our paths will cross, but right now, I'm going to look for Arliss Padgett."

\*\*\*

Since Padgett may or may not be in Virginia, I decided to check with my usual sources in town first. After leaving the bar, I called Janice Chan, owner of my favorite hot dog restaurant. Janice said Arliss used to come around and scrounge in the trash cans until she chased him off.

"He'd even grab up the fries and bread crumbs people threw out for the birds, if you can believe that. I felt sorry for him at first, but then he really started being a nuisance. I haven't seen him in a long time."

"Throw out some stale buns."

"Very funny, Randall."

Next I called Bilby Foster at his pawn shop. Bilby knew who Arliss Padgett was, too, and said the man wasn't allowed anywhere near his shop.

"Caught him trying to steal a microwave. Not only was he a shoplifter, he was a stupid one. Have you ever seen somebody try to hide a microwave oven under his jacket?"

My go-to reference librarian Mandy didn't know him. "That's okay," I said. "From what other people have told me, he sounds like the kind of guy who wouldn't come into the library unless he needed a warm place to sleep."

I stopped by the Red Cross and other shelters for the homeless. No one knew Arliss Padgett. I was going to have to go to Virginia, damn it.

I was walking to my car when a voice shouted, "Hey! Hey, you!"

A man approached, his face red with anger. It was Garrett Henderson, my last deadbeat dad. He was about my age but had gotten fat and spotty, like a pumpkin left too long in the field, too rotten for pie, too lumpy for a jack-o'-lantern.

Henderson got right in my face. "I been looking for you. You oughta mind your own business instead of hassling honest hard-working men like myself."

I did not need this aggravation. "Look," I said, "if you're so honest and hard-working, how come you skipped out to Vegas and gambled away your family's money? Don't you think your little girls would like something besides soup for dinner once in a while?"

"You don't know what the hell you're talking about."

"I know what your wife told me. You hadn't paid her alimony or child support in months. She had to go to the food bank or a church to get enough food. Was she lying?"

"Stupid cow. I had a run of bad luck, that's all. No need to call out some two-bit PI."

"Aren't you due in court this week?"

I wouldn't have believed Henderson's face could get any redder, but it did. I started to walk away. He grabbed my arm.

"She never should've hired you. If I see you following me again, I'll kick your ass."

"You'd have to be following me to do that, but I get your drift." I gave him an elbow jab into his soft pumpkin belly. "I'd think twice about that if I were you."

He groaned as he doubled up. "You ain't seen the last of me," he squeaked.

"Oh, I think I have."

*I hope I have*, I thought. The last thing I wanted was for this sad case to continue.

I was driving home, listening to the New Black Eagle Jazz Band tear through a high-powered rendition of "Jersey Lightning," when the CD player crackled with an unusual burst of static. Then a clear voice said, "David Randall."

I'm surprised I didn't jerk the car off the road. I slowed down and pulled into the nearest parking lot, a funeral home, of all things. Perfect.

"David Randall."

The voice didn't sound like Lindsey. "Yes," I said, wondering what was happening in the Great Beyond now. The last time a spirit tried to contact me she came in over the TV. "Who is this? What do you want?"

"Justice," the clear voice said.

"How can I help you?" Another burst of static drowned the reply. I turned up the volume, but the voice was gone and "Jersey Lightning" popped back on. Okay. Justice. Kind of vague. Maybe the spirit should've used my cell phone. Even though this was an odd occurrence, I knew from experience if the message was important, my departed clients would get back to me via Lindsey. That was something I looked forward to.

# Chapter Four

## *"Papa, Better Watch Your Step"*

B y the time I got home, Kary was with one of her piano students, and I had to wait until the lesson was over to tell her about my case and my latest close encounter.

After the student did a proper massacre of "Down in the Valley" and received a gold star sticker, he left, looking relieved. Kary joined me in the island. She sat down in her favorite chair, a little rocking chair with a red velvet cushion. I handed her a Diet Coke and took my seat in the faded blue arm chair. "Everything go okay at school today?"

"Frustrating news." She still had on her school clothes, a neat denim skirt, a bright yellow blouse, and earrings shaped like little crayons, School Teacher Chic. With her long silky blond hair and warm brown eyes, Kary could make any outfit look good. She tucked a strand of her hair behind one perfect ear, making the little crayon earring dance. "The state requires a Bachelor's and a Master's degree in order to qualify for Licensure as a guidance counselor. Well, I found out today, PCC doesn't offer all the classes I need."

Kary had recently decided that as much as she loved teaching elementary kids, her true calling might be in guidance. She'd started taking evening classes at Parkland Community College. It was a bigger project than she anticipated.

"How about Charlotte or Greensboro?"

"That would involve a commute, and you know Turbo is fine to get around town, but that little car isn't up to hours of interstate driving. Plus if I work all day and drive to classes at night that leaves me zero time to help you with your cases."

Kary was always up for a mystery and was excellent help, especially if the case involved a disguise.

"Then I have just the thing to cheer you up," I said. "Come hit the Westville, Virginia, flea market with me on Saturday. All expenses paid. I need to snoop around."

"That sounds delightful."

"First thing tomorrow morning before all the good stuff gets gone. You could do some Christmas shopping."

"What are you looking for?"

"Another deadbeat dad."

Kary knows how I feel about that kind of case. "Oh. Sorry. Nothing else right now?"

"I did hear from the Great Beyond." Before I could explain further, Lottie scurried in.

"Oh, Kary, I'm so glad you're home! I wonder if you could read this and tell me what you think." She handed her a stack of papers. "Do you have time? I really want to finish the haystack scene tonight."

"Of course," Kary said. "David, you can fill me in later."

I was not happy to have my Kary time usurped, but "later" meant snuggled up in bed together, so I could wait.

Noises in the kitchen told me Camden was fixing dinner. He started around the corner, saw Lottie, and quickly backed away. I gave him a look and wiggled one elbow to indicate that he was chicken. He touched his nose. No psychic brainwaves needed for that little exchange. Lottie sat down on the sofa and watched anxiously as Kary read.

After a few minutes, Kary looked up. "This is very interesting, Lottie, but I think some of the pages are out of order."

"Oh, no, that's to indicate Randolph's confusion. He's not sure where he is."

I couldn't resist. "Isn't he in a haystack?"

"No, the treasure is hidden in the haystack."

"Do people still stack hay? I thought most farmers rolled it into bales."

Lottie gave me a startled look. "That changes everything! Oh, my goodness. If the treasure is in one of those hay balls, then the villains could roll it down a hill."

"And into a lake."

Lottie took the papers from Kary and the pencil from behind her ear and began to scribble on the top page. "That's wonderful! That will work perfectly." She ran back up the stairs.

Kary watched her go with the fond smile she has for her little students. "I'm so glad she's excited about her work. She's going to help me out, too. Did she tell you?"

"No. Help you with what?" Kary's eyes gleamed with the fervor I'd learned to recognize although I couldn't imagine how scattered little Lottie could help her adopt a child. To my relief, this was something else.

"She has a friend who works with social services, and it's possible I can sit in on some of their guidance sessions. Lottie said she'd put in a good word for me. She said she wanted to do something to thank me, even though of course I told her she didn't have to. I might even be able to talk to some of the young girls at the Planned Parenthood clinic. That's something I'm still working out for myself."

Due to an unplanned pregnancy in her teens, Kary had lost a baby and her ability to have children. This was her way of coping. She'd leapt over countless mental hurdles to be able to deal with this.

I was glad Lottie was good for something, but I didn't want her to get all the credit for keeping Kary happy. "About the case," I said, which immediately got her attention.

"Oh, yes. A deadbeat dad, you said."

"Doreen, the young woman who hired me, is eighteen and works at the Quik-Fry. Her parents are divorced and he's not keeping up with his alimony. We need to find him so she and her mom can pay the rent. His name is Arliss Padgett."

"We have some Padgetts at school. I'll ask around. Anything else?"

"Not right now."

"Well, keep me in the loop."

I'd learned long ago this was the wisest thing to do.

She stood and smoothed her skirt. "Time to get out of these school clothes," she said. "Then I want to hear about your latest message from Beyond."

Kary went upstairs to change. Seeing the coast was clear of Lottie, Camden came around to the island.

"When does Ellin get back?" I asked him.

"She said Thursday. Her birthday is the eighteenth, and I promised to take her out to dinner, plus there's some sort of fifteen-year class reunion she wants to go to."

Class Reunion. The Royal Bitch Academy, no doubt. "She's dragging you to one of those? You know you'll have to perform. Here's my amazing psychic husband." Every time Ellin cons him into attending a social function, he ends up telling futures all night.

He sat down on the sofa. "I promised her I'd go, and that's one promise that's easy to keep."

"Okay. Just be prepared to wander through fifteen years of remorse and envy." I picked up the remote and channel surfed until I found *2001: A Space Odyssey*. The space travelers were jogging hamster-style around the inside of their wheel-like ship. "Maybe that's what I should try."

"Jogging?"

"Astronaut."

Camden gave me one of his long stares, the kind that make me feel he's opened a door in my brain and made himself at home. "Seriously, what do you want to do?"

"Thought I'd open a bar downtown."

"You don't want to do that." Countless times Camden's heard me say I would never follow in my bartender father's footsteps and spend my life listening to other peoples' problems. I ended up doing that, anyway, just without the beer.

"Well, you tell me what I want."

"You want to help Doreen."

"Already said I would."

"You want Kary to be Mrs. Randall."

"Yep."

He paused, as if that door to my brain had warped a little and was hard to open. "And you want to keep everyone safe. No more accidents."

Since that was exactly what I was thinking, I wasn't going to argue. "I don't see how tracking down these deadbeat dads fits into my cosmic plan, do you?"

"You're just cranky because you're in a slump."

I started to tell him what I thought of this when Kary returned wearing jeans and a light blue sweatshirt, her hair pulled back in a ponytail.

"Hi, guys. Is dinner ready?"

Camden jumped up. "Sorry, Kary. I got distracted by Randall's mid-life crisis."

Her smile was impish. "I don't think he's quite reached mid-life yet. Need some help with dinner?"

"No, thanks. I got it."

She sat down in her chair and turned to me. "You started to tell me something about the Great Beyond before Lottie interrupted."

"I had another spirit try to call in on my car radio. It wants justice."

"Don't we all."

"I'll be glad when everyone over there gets their signals straight."

"It means another dream from Lindsey, doesn't it? That's always good."

"Yes, and she let me know in no uncertain terms I was to help Doreen. I heard her loud and clear. So I expect she'll tell me what this other spirit wants. Besides, what else has been going on around here except supernatural business? We've had all sorts of ghosts, cursed objects, talking snakes, and we never know what Camden's talent is going to morph into."

"I heard that," he called from the kitchen.

"Float our dinner out here, will you?"

He made a rude reply, and Kary grinned as she got up. "No need to move anything, Cam. I'll set the table."

# Chapter Five

## *"Poor Papa"*

Saturday was a beautiful clear day, about fifty-five degrees. It never gets really cold and wintry in North Carolina until January or February, and sometimes there's no snow at all. This November was cool and clear as glass. The last of the leaves were clinging to bare branches, little tattered red and gold flags. In our yard, most of the leaves on the huge old oak trees immediately turned brown. Some made a half-hearted attempt at gold, but they were such ancient trees, I could just imagine the leaves saying, "Change color again? Damn, forget this. I'm just gonna die and fall off." They fell off by the thousands. Camden spent days raking them into massive piles that the wind blew all over the neighborhood and eventually back to our yard.

Today's sky was a hard bright blue with just enough snap in the air to make Kary's cheeks pink. Not that she needed any enhancement. She looked great in her jeans, dark green sweater over a gold turtleneck, and dark green hat. I wanted to stand there and look at her the rest of the day, to hell with Arliss Padgett and the rest of the world.

First we dropped Camden off at Tamara's Boutique. Then on our drive to the Westville flea market I explained our mission.

"Padgett sounds like a real charmer," Kary said. "How are you going to make him pay up?"

"I have an idea how to catch him."

"But your heart's not really into this, is it?"

Sometimes I forget that there's more than one perceptive person in the house. "Have you been taking lessons from Camden?"

"I know you'd rather be working on something bigger and more important, but if you can help this girl—"

"I'm not sure finding her worthless father is going to help anything."

"Okay, I don't have to be Cam to see that you're in a bad mood."

"No, no." I didn't want my perfect Saturday with Kary to implode. "I'm not in a bad mood."

"You don't think finding this girl's father is important enough?"

"Yes, but—"

She didn't let me finish. "You've found valuable music, several murderers, some irreplaceable Art Nouveau, and, what was that other thing? Oh, yes, Rufus's baby girl. I don't want to hear any more of this talk."

"But those cases were few and far between. Meanwhile, I'm stuck tracking down runaway parents."

"Who says you have to do that?"

"It pays the bills. Don't you do an occasional pageant for the money? As I recall, you're not too fond of that."

She paused. "Okay, you've got me there."

I turned off the highway onto the service road that led to the flea market. It took a while to find a parking place, but eventually I squeezed the Fury between an ancient pickup truck and a Volkswagen covered in bumper stickers. Then Kary and I walked into the wonder that was the Westville Flea Market.

I'm not exactly sure what inspires people to say, "I think I'll put all my useless junk out on a table and see who buys it," but from the looks of the market, everyone in that corner of Virginia was inspired that day. Festive yard sale colors brightened the tables in disheartening shades of brown, avocado, orange, and mustard yellow. Even when this stuff was new, it was ugly.

"Speaking of ugly." I took out the driver's license Doreen had given me. "Okay, partner, here's what we're looking for."

"My goodness," she said. "That's a distinctive face."

A distinctive face we didn't see as we made our way through the booths. Nor had anyone seen Padgett.

Kary looked through the offerings on one vendor's table and held up a wreath made of bent twigs and straw. "What do you think? For Angie and Rufus, to go on the door of their new house."

"Looks fine to me."

"I really wish they'd been able to keep Mary Rose."

Mary Rose was Rufus's baby girl. Since being a father had not been on his list of things to do, he and Angie decided they weren't quite ready for a baby. Kary, of course, had hoped Mary Rose would stay in the neighborhood.

"I'm sure they'll figure it out," I said. "With the new house and Angie looking for more work, it was too much."

"Oh, I know they will."

On the next table, Kary found some white pencils printed with black music notes. "These are perfect for my piano students. Help me find fourteen of them."

I put the wreath on my arm and helped her count out fourteen pencils. "What about your kids at school?"

"We have erasers shaped like Santa for them."

The toothless geezer selling the pencils was so taken by Kary he tossed an extra pencil into the bag. "In case you break one," he said with a leer.

"Have you seen Arliss Padgett?" I asked him, but his eyes were on Kary and he barely glanced at the driver's license.

"Nah. Never heard of him."

"Thanks, anyway," I told him as I steered her away.

Kary paused by a booth selling stacks of video tapes. "Do people still use these?"

"You'd be surprised," the vendor said. She was a plump woman holding a one-eyed cat. "I sell loads of them here. Looking for anything in particular?"

"We're looking for a friend of ours, Arliss Padgett."

The woman shook her head. "Don't know him. How 'bout a cat? This one here's for sale. Only got one good eye, but he's a snuggler."

The cat looked bored and anything but snuggly.

"No, thank you," Kary said. "We've got two at home."

"Change your mind, I'll be here all day."

"Doesn't look like we're having much success," Kary said as we walked on.

"At least you're finding some Christmas presents."

"Has Cam said anything about what he'd like for Christmas?"

"Probably some more books on UFOs."

"We may not find those here, but you never know." She looked over the next table full of green glass vases, the kind florists use. We had at least ten in a kitchen cabinet. "What do you want for Christmas?"

I'm looking at it, I wanted to say. "Oh, socks, ties, the usual."

"I wish your mother could join us this year."

"She's going on a cruise with some of her friends."

I thought of the extravagant Christmas holidays my parents always planned. My mother would start cooking the day after Thanksgiving: cookies, candy, peanut brittle. The house would be outlined in lights and covered with decorations, including a plastic Santa and reindeer on the roof. I always got everything on my list, and sometimes Dad would dress up as Santa and go through our little town of Elbert Falls, giving candy and toys to all the kids. In Minnesota, a white Christmas was a given. Couldn't count on it here. A small price to pay to spend Christmas with Kary.

We wound our way through more tables and booths. Kary bought a basket for one of her girlfriends, something shaped like an apple for the teacher she worked with, a box of candles, and dishcloths she assured me were perfect for the kitchen, although I objected to the cow motif. All these purchases fit into the basket, which I dutifully hauled around.

While Kary was examining some sad looking chairs, I asked the man behind the table if he'd seen Arliss Padgett lately.

"Padgett? Nope. Ain't seen him lately."

"Is he usually around?"

"Usually. What you want him for? I don't mind telling you he'll cheat you blind. He's one sorry bastard."

I gave him one of my cards. "Sorry or not, he's come into a lot of money. I represent an agency that specializes in inheritances.

Mr. Padgett's cousin made a generous provision for him in his will. He'd probably like to know about it."

The vendor squinted at the card. I have several different kinds. This one said, "David H. Randall, Inheritance Specialist" and had my phone number on it. I didn't know what the hell that meant, but neither did anyone else.

"You say Arliss is coming into some money?"

"Yes, quite a lot. I was told I could find him here."

The vendor rubbed his nose. "Tell you what. I'll spread the word. He owes everybody in Virginia. Sooner he gets this money the sooner we can beat it out of his worthless hide."

"Sounds like the perfect plan. Let me give you a few more cards, and you can spread them around, too."

After sprinkling cards among the vendors, Kary and I loaded her treasures into the Fury and started home. For lunch we stopped at a diner called Papa Jud's. The food was what one would expect from a place called Papa Jud's, corn bread, collard greens, and pintos, but no one there had any information on Padgett. Kary had a make-up lesson for one of her students who'd been sick, so we had to get back to town. I dropped her off at the student's house and offered to stay, but she assured me the little girl's folks would give her a ride home.

*** 

Before heading back to Grace Street, I decided to swing by Tamara's Boutique  to see if Camden needed a ride home. He had a cell phone, but he rarely had it with him, so I didn't bother to call. I was surprised when Tamara told me Camden had already left.

"You didn't need him today?"

"I didn't want him today. He was in such a mood."

Tamara was a gorgeous brunette with exotic green eyes. Her clothing store was filled with expensive slivers of material she calls dresses and all the glittery accessories women like to buy, like pocketbooks and belts and jewelry. Tamara had on a slinky blue number with little round mirrors along the neckline that winked when she moved.

"Brooding about his evil powers?"

"Something like that. He seemed so distracted, I finally told him to go home. One of the regular customers gave him a ride. What's up, David? He's not taking those pills again, is he?"

"No. Jordan's asked him to help find a serial killer."

"This isn't the same killer I've been reading about, is it?"

"Yes, that's the one."

"Are you on the case, too?"

"No, I've got a few other things to do." No need to go into detail with Tamara. "When did you send Camden home?"

"About an hour ago."

I'd better see what was up. Hopefully it wasn't anything breakable.

# Chapter Six

### *"Look Out, Papa"*

At home, I found Camden washing the dishes, an activity he said calmed him down. He didn't look calm. He looked distracted. I got a Coke from the fridge and sat down at the counter. "Tamara says you left work in what Rufus would call a conniption fit. Did Jordan come by with something else for you to feel?

He shook his head. "I couldn't concentrate. I kept seeing that creepy guy's hands fondling all that hair."

"Did you see the creepy guy's face?"

"No. That would've been too useful." He dried his hands and pushed his hair out of his eyes. "Why don't you find this serial killer and solve both our problems?"

"Maybe Arliss Padgett is the killer. That would be ideal." I chugged the rest of my cola and tossed the empty can into the recycle bin by the back door. "You want to come with me on an Arliss hunt?"

He hung the dishcloth over the edge of the sink. "No, thanks. I promised Angie I'd finish her cabinets today."

"We're not going over there until later, right? What else have you got to do?"

He sat down at the counter across from me. "I'm still concerned about my reaction to that blouse."

"You've had worse."

"Yes, but something about that—I don't know. I'd rather stay out of this one."

"Seriously, do you think you can?"

He found a stray penny on the counter and put it in the grocery frog, a ceramic frog-shaped dish that held all our loose change. "Probably not."

"Come help me find Arliss Padgett, then."

"I just have this feeling something really bad is going to happen, and Arliss is part of it."

"All the more reason to find him."

His attention was all on the frog. "Not right now."

"Then give me a call when you're ready."

I left him deciding what to do and went out to the Fury with every intention of scouring the city for Pa Padgett and reporting back to Doreen. The Fury had other ideas. She refused to crank. I was under the hood, scowling and poking, when Terrance "Toad" Hall drove up in his taxi, Old Betsy. Toad's tall, thin, and elegant, but his driving habits are unorthodox, so he's nicknamed for that manic frog from *Wind in the Willows*.

"Need a ride, partner?"

"How'd you guess?"

He laughed. "I just brought Mr. Matheson home and thought I'd swing by. What's wrong with the Fury?"

I started to say she'd given up, like me, but decided that sounded too pathetic. I straightened and wiped my hands on the towel I kept in the car. "Needs a new battery."

"Want a lift to the service station?"

"That'd be great, thanks."

I got in the taxi's front passenger side, admired the latest string of beads hanging from the rear view mirror, and checked to see if the hula girls were still swaying in the back. They were. "Did Matheson actually speak to you?"

"He said, 'Four oh three Temple.'"

"I've never heard him say anything." The Mathesons' property was in back of Camden's. I'd seen Mrs. Matheson once. They were ninja neighbors.

Toad drove up Grace and made a right onto Food Row. "You

know Arliss Padgett?" I asked.

Toad grimaced. "Oh, yes. A wretched man. Had me bring him in all the way from that trailer park he lives in, then stiffed me on the fare. Rolled right out of the cab and ran up the street. I hope he's wanted for something really grotesque."

"Same old stuff. He's left his family in the lurch. The daughter hired me to find him, but I doubt we'll get anything out of him. He sounds like a career bum."

"That creature has a family? Sad news."

"Yeah, all the families I've been involved with lately have been sad news."

Toad stopped for a red light, turned and faced me. "You don't have to always find these awful fathers. You could say no. Keep out of domestic cases."

"Deadbeat dads are my specialty."

"Who says?"

I thought of Buddy, spreading the news far and wide, and how Doreen had seen this as the last opportunity to find her worthless father. "Apparently everybody."

The light changed and Toad drove to the Super Gas on the corner. I picked out a battery, paid with my credit card, and got back in the cab. Toad's cell phone affixed to the dashboard gave a little beep and a female voice told him to go to Emerald and Fourth.

"Roger that." He turned to me. "Anywhere else you need to go?"

"No, thanks."

He took me home and drove off, hula girls and beads swaying. I replaced the battery, and this time the Fury decided she'd roar to life. I drove out to Springdale Trailer Park, hoping to chat with Doreen's mother or neighbors to see if any of them had a clue where Arliss might be lurking.

The trailer park was alive with the red and blue flashing lights of police cars and an ambulance. For one heart-stopping moment, I thought Doreen might have been injured or dead. I caught a glimpse of a woman being hauled onto a stretcher. She was older than Doreen, limp and white, and her head looked like a peeled tomato.

Jordan was standing with a group of policemen and residents. He scowled at me. "What the hell are you doing here?"

"My client lives here. Doreen Padgett."

His scowl deepened. He motioned with a small lift of his chin to the woman being questioned by his partner. "That's Hazel Padgett. She found the body."

Doreen's mother was an older, graying version of Doreen, the waistline of her faded print dress up around her armpits, her skinny legs circled by thick wrinkled hose. She eyed the policeman with distrust.

"Didn't see nothing. Didn't hear nothing. Just found her."

"When was this, Mrs. Padgett?"

"Nigh onto noon or thereabouts. I come out to tend to my laundry."

An unappealing array of dingy clothes and socks sagged on a line strung between two poles. Hazel Padgett pointed to a spot underneath the clothesline.

"There she was. Thought she's sick, 'cause she don't drink none. Then I seen her head."

I'd seen her head, too, and it wasn't something I ever wanted to see again. "Did she have blond hair?" I asked.

Mrs. Padgett nodded. Jordan took my arm and despite my protest, steered me away.

"She's my client's mother," I said. "I came out here to talk to her."

"Not now, Randall. She's a witness."

"But isn't this the work of your serial killer?"

Jordan's expression was stony. "Maybe. Maybe not."

"Were the other victims scalped like that?"

"No. Our man's more careful."

"Maybe he's progressed. Regressed, I should say."

Jordan took out his cigarettes. "I don't like this. You're looking for Padgett and we have a copycat murder right in his backyard."

"He's the killer. Solves both our cases all at once."

"Nothing's that easy." He sighed and came to a decision. "All right. What have you got?"

"I spent this morning at the Westville Market just over the state line. The vendors all know Padgett because he owes them money. I handed out some of my business cards and told them Padgett's come into a sizable inheritance. I'm hoping that'll lure him out."

"An inheritance?"

"Works every time."

Jordan blew a long stream of smoke. "If he contacts you, I want to know."

"Same here. Now I want to talk to Mrs. Padgett." When he looked like he was going to say no, I said, "You want Camden to check on this murder, too, don't you? You may need an interpreter."

After considering this, he relented. "Two minutes."

Hazel Padgett gave me the same narrow suspicious stare she'd given the policemen. "Mrs. Padgett, I'm David Randall. Your daughter Doreen hired me to find your husband."

She crossed her skinny arms under her drooping chest. "She told me. Thought it was a waste of money myself. You found him?"

"Not yet. I thought you could help me."

She turned her head to spit into the dirt. "Useless."

I didn't know if she meant me or Arliss. "When was the last time you saw him?"

"Hadn't seen him for weeks now. Doreen, she does her best to help me. I told her hiring somebody wouldn't do no good. Him and me's been divorced for nigh on a year now, and I ain't seen hardly any of the money he's supposed to give me."

"Does he have any particular place he likes to go? A bar? A friend's house?"

"He don't have no friends. Hangs around flea markets mostly, trying to steal things to sell."

"Did he know the woman who was killed?"

She indicated the people watching from the sidelines. "Everybody knew Pauline Raterman. Everybody knows everybody around here."

"Is Arliss Padgett capable of murder?"

She took a long moment before she answered. "Well, when he was drunk, he used to knock me around some, and he beat on

Doreen one time when she sassed him. I don't know that he'd skin somebody's head like that, though. Don't seem likely." She watched as the policemen put yellow tape around the murder scene. "Now everybody'll be looking for him, that's for sure. Might as well give me back Doreen's money. Let the cops get him, put him in jail. That's where he belongs anyway."

"I'll ask Doreen what she wants me to do."

She wanted to argue this point, but Jordan called me away. "Clear out, Randall. We've got work to do."

I got into the Fury and sat for a while, staring at the bleak trailers, the dirt roads, the little groups of curious neighbors. *I have a feeling something really bad is going to happen, and Arliss is part of it.* Isn't that what Camden told me? As usual, he was exactly right. But what reason would Arliss Padgett have for killing Pauline Raterman? With his history of domestic violence, a more likely victim would have been his wife or his daughter. I couldn't see this as a crime of passion, and from the look of things, I could rule out money, jewels, and famous paintings. Jordan was probably right. This could be the work of a copycat, someone who didn't have quite enough mercury in his thermometer, to borrow one of Rufus's colorful Southern sayings.

# Chapter Seven

*"Papa Was a Rolling Stone"*

When I got home, Camden was out on the front porch feeding his werewolf. This latest stray was a large, extremely hairy, mentally challenged man, always growling and scratching around for a handout. Camden said his name was Tom, but I'd never heard Tom say anything remotely intelligible. I guess Camden remembered men like this from his own hobo days. No doubt there was a secret sign somewhere on a fence that said, "If you're riding the rails through Parkland, 302 Grace is the place to stop for a sandwich."

As I got out of the car, Tom grabbed his food and a can of Coke, ready to run.

"It's okay," Camden said. "It's Randall. You remember him."

Tom's eyes beamed small and dark from his forest of hair. He said something that sounded like "Urrrhh," and scurried across the yard to hide behind a tree.

"Nice to see you again, Tom," I said.

"He's been helping me rake the leaves," Camden said. Tom wouldn't take food unless he did a chore to pay for it.

"Haven't seen him lately. Been visiting his relatives in Sasquatch Town?"

"He's been at the shelter in Tranquil Grove, but he didn't like it. I've been trying to explain that he can't catch a ride with the trains the way he used to. Come have a seat. He'll be okay."

Camden sat down in the porch swing, and I sat down in one of the rocking chairs. Tom peered around the tree like Bigfoot deciding which camper to eat. There were several cans of soda and a pile of sandwiches on the wicker table between the rocking chairs.

"Can I have one of these, or are they all for Tom?"

"Help yourself."

"Does he know how to share?"

I got a dark look for a reply. With Tom watching my every move, I chose a sandwich and a Coke, expecting him to hurl himself at the porch to defend his food supply. When he stayed put, I raised my sandwich in salute.

"Come up and join us, Tom."

To my surprise, he came around the tree and slowly walked up to the porch steps, where he sat down, his eyes still wary, and finished his lunch.

"Is anyone else here?" I asked Camden.

"Kary went downtown to the South Avenue Clinic, and Lottie's rewriting something she calls the windmill scene." He stopped eating and gave me a power stare. "What's happened?"

"You were right about something bad happening. There's been another murder, one of Doreen's neighbors."

"The same killer?"

"I think so. It could very well be Arliss Padgett. Don't be surprised if Jordan comes by with another piece of something for you to hold."

As I said this, Jordan's patrol car pulled up. Tom took off, a hairy blur disappearing around the house.

Jordan got out. "What the hell was that?"

"Camden's werewolf," I said.

"Save it, Randall." He took a worn brown shoe from a paper bag. "Cam, if you don't mind. We've got another murder victim."

I could tell Camden did mind, but he got up and set his Coke aside. He touched the shoe and immediately zoned out. He turned three shades whiter and started breathing hard quick breaths. When I reached over to take the shoe, he shook his head.

"Wait. A few more minutes. I can't—" He dropped the shoe, groped for the porch swing, and sat down. "Good lord."

Jordan and I both asked if he was okay. He nodded. He took a drink and caught his breath.

"My God. Her head."

"Is it the same man you saw before?" Jordan asked.

He took a few more moments before he could reply. "Yes, but there was something different about him this time. Much more violent. Almost as if he were trying to prove something. I still can't see his face." He rubbed his eyes. "Sorry. The images were so sudden."

Jordan took the shoe. "Maybe later?"

I could tell Camden didn't want to have anything more to do with Pauline Raterman's shoe. "Maybe."

"We'll call you," I said to Jordan.

He caught my eye and correctly interpreted the message: Enough for now. He thanked Camden for his assistance, got in his car, and drove off. A few minutes later, Tom came around the corner of the house and stood looking at the sandwiches. Camden didn't seem to notice him, so I handed Tom the plate. He frowned a hairy frown as if I'd committed a social *faux pas* and carefully picked one sandwich from the pile.

"Pardon me," I said. "I'm not up on hobo etiquette."

He frowned another frown at Camden and then glared up the road after Jordan. Probably remembering an unpleasant run-in with the law.

"You okay?" I asked Camden.

He took another drink of Coke. "Add one more unforgettable image to my repertoire."

"I saw her, too. What did you mean about this one being different?"

"It was the same guy, but not for the same purpose. He didn't need her hair, he just took it."

"Compulsively, you mean?"

"I don't know. He's using all the hair he's collected for something. I can't tell what. But he killed this poor woman just for the hell of it."

"Because he could, maybe?"

Camden looked off into space. I knew he was seeing Pauline's badly skinned head because I was, too. "Something else." He sighed in exasperation. "If I'm not going to get a clear picture, then why get a picture, at all?"

"Something will come up."

"Stupid freaking talent."

Tom had been listening, his little eyes going back and forth between us.

"You need another drink, Tom?" Camden asked.

He shook his head and made a growling noise.

"We're going over to Rufus and Angie's new house. You want to come?"

Another growl.

"See you later, then."

Tom loped off. I waited until he was out of sight. "I hate to say this, but are you sure Tom isn't our killer? He looks like someone who'd have a hair fetish."

"Our killer is a lot less civilized than Tom."

I thought again of Pauline Raterman's head. "I have to agree. Tell Jordan this is too much."

"I can manage. Ellie will be home in a few days, and that'll help."

Thanks to having no psychic ability, at all, Ellin was able to blank out the more disturbing images from his mind. But she wasn't here, and I'd be no help in this situation. I pushed myself out of the rocking chair. "Well, since we're both feeling useless, let's go over and help Rufus and Angie get settled in their new place."

***

The rest of the afternoon was spent at Rufus and Angie's new abode two streets over from Grace on River Street, a white two-story house with black shutters. All of the houses in that part of Parkland were old with distinctive features. The walkway had a patchwork pattern of different colored stones, and there was a wishing well in the back yard, a nice-sized space with maple trees. Their bright yellow leaves were scattered everywhere. The roof had an interesting scalloped edge, which Camden had already repaired. All that remained were the kitchen cabinets.

While Camden and Rufus worked in the kitchen, Camden sang "O Holy Night" followed by Rufus adding a chorus of "Grandma Got Run Over by a Reindeer."

I helped Angie rearrange furniture in the living room. "Guys," she said, "enough with the Christmas carols. It's not even Thanksgiving yet."

They ignored her plea and continued their early holiday concert from the sublime to the ridiculous. When the cabinets were finished and Angie had the living room the way she wanted it, we had takeout pizza on the floor, picnic style, along with Parkland's beverage of choice, Mountain Dew.

Rufus and Angie took up one whole side of the room. Rufus was pro wrestler size with a scraggly red beard and ever-present baseball cap. Angie was also full-figured. I liked them a lot. They'd even helped on a couple of cases. But their sheer size, their thundering footsteps, the amount of food they inhaled—it had been like living with a pair of wooly mammoths.

Angie's wide jeans and even wider tee shirt were splattered with paint. Her tiny eyes gleamed like bright beads. "You guys have been very helpful, thanks."

"We aim to please," Rufus said, his mouth full of pizza. "So, what've we got? One more room to paint, windows to wash, we're done?"

"We're done," Angie said.

He peeled another slice of pizza out of the cardboard box. "How's your case coming along, Randall? You found Doreen's old man yet?"

"Not yet, but I am on the trail. The next time you see Buddy, tell him to please keep his charity cases to a minimum."

"Hell, he knew you could do it."

"Doing it's no problem. Wanting to do it is another thing."

He grinned. "You don't like bringing these useless dads to justice?"

"It's my sole purpose in life." I scooped up a piece of pepperoni before it hit the floor. "What do you know about Arliss

Padgett?"

"Not much."

"Is he likely to be hanging around town, or drifting from state to state?"

"Don't think he'd have the resources to go too far, and from what little I know about him, he's more a follower than a leader. Likes to insinuate himself with the big dogs."

"'Insinuate.' That's a good one, Rufus."

"Better give me twenty points."

Camden and I had created a game called Vocabulary Challenge, a game that started when my first divorce left me sole owner of a Word a Day calendar. Rufus often surprised us with an impressive word of his own.

He chugged his Mountain Dew. "When's your sweetie coming home?" he asked Camden.

"Thursday. The eighteenth's her birthday."

"Been mighty quiet around your house, I'll bet."

"She still after you to move?" Angie asked.

He sighed as he took another piece of pizza. "Yeah, she has her heart set on one of those Colonial style mausoleums in Starwood. I told her we'd go have a look."

"Hell," Rufus said, "she oughta be happy as a goat eating briars now that Angie and me are out of her way. 'Cept for that squirrely little woman, you practically got the whole place to yourselves." He chugged a second Mountain Dew and burped heartily. "Well, me and my gal here sure love our new place, don't we, sugar lips?" He gave Angie an affectionate pat on the arm that sounded like a stone slapping water and sent her arm fat quivering.

She gave his beard a playful tug. "You bet. Need some more Dew, lover boy?"

She started up and Camden said, "No, no, I'll get it. Be right back."

As he disappeared around the corner to the kitchen, Rufus leaned over toward me and spoke in a low voice. "He ain't very cheerful tonight. You involved in some other weird case?"

Sometimes I forgot a shrewd mind lurked behind all the face fuzz. "Jordan had him feel some murder victim's clothes earlier today."

"Damn. Thought he wasn't going to do that kind of thing anymore."

At Rufus's lowering brow, I added, "It was no big deal. He got a few impressions, that's all."

Camden returned, carrying several cans of soda. He handed one to Angie. "Here you go."

Rufus scowled. "What the hell is all this about a murder victim?"

"Just feeling something for Jordan." He sat down and gave me a scowl of his own. "Which I don't want to go into."

"He beat it out of me," I said.

"You ought not to do that kind of crap and you know it," Rufus told him.

"Even when it could help catch a killer? What good is this stupid talent if I don't use it to help people?"

"What good are you if you go off the deep end? Next thing you know, you'll be sending pizza slices dancing around the room."

"I'll send you dancing around the room if you don't back off."

Rufus guffawed and nearly choked on his Mountain Dew. "Makes you wonder what's next, though, don't it?"

Camden shook his head. "I worry about that all the time."

"All the more reason not to go around feeling stuff!" Rufus said, as if he'd won the argument.

The argument was far from over. "Look," Camden said, "if I could get rid of all this psychic ability, I would. If I could wake up one morning and not have any more visions, I'd be delighted. But it's not going to happen. So I might as well help Jordan and anyone else who asks me."

Angie had been quiet, munching her pizza. Now she spoke. "So who's the killer?"

"A very disturbed man," Camden said. "He's obsessed with women's long blond hair."

She grinned and tugged her short brown hair. "Guess I'm safe, huh?"

I'd like to see the man who'd try to tackle Angie.

"You're not going to become this guy, are you?" was her next question, "like that songwriter fellow?"

Occasionally, a spirit likes to park itself in Camden, which adds a special dimension to my cases.

"No," Camden said. "I just tuned in for a minute."

Rufus tossed his empty can into the recycling bin. "Don't like it. Could mess up your mind."

Camden looked off in the distance. I wondered if he was wishing he had another bottle of vision-suppressing headache pills, or if he was planning some other way to not be psychic. "No more than it already is."

***

Later, we walked home. I was warm enough in my Minnesota Vikings sweatshirt. Camden had on his blue jean jacket and a multicolored scarf Kary had knitted for him. When the nights got cold and windy, he usually wore the scarf to protect his voice.

"I have an idea," I said. "You be the detective and I'll be the psychic. We haven't had the episode yet where we switch bodies."

He looked up at the clear sky. "Doesn't lightning have to strike?"

"Or some weird experiment goes horribly awry. Or we find an alien artifact no one's supposed to touch."

He kept his gaze on the few stars visible through the glare of Food Row's garish signs. When he gets that look, I know he's thinking of his mysterious father. He's convinced Dad's vehicle of choice was a UFO. So far, I hadn't found any evidence to the contrary.

He brought his gaze back to earth. "I'm worried about this serial killer."

"Is it Arliss?"

"I can't tell. I don't think so."

We turned the corner of Willow Street and walked down Grace. We stopped in front of 302. The house looked warm and inviting. Yellow squares of light beamed from the windows, and the porch light attracted a few remaining silvery moths. The breeze rearranged the leaves, getting them ready for their next mad dash across the yard. I could see our black and white cat Oreo curled up next to the lamp on my desk and the brightly colored sun catchers shaped like butterflies twinkling in Kary's upstairs window.

Camden said, "Everything I care about is in there."

I felt pretty much the same way. "But Ellin would rather live in Starwood."

"I understand having other people around is distracting to her, but I don't understand why she doesn't like the house. I've always felt very calm and safe here."

Since moving to Parkland, Camden had always lived at 302 Grace. Even with all the various tenants moving in and out, the house had a good feel to it. Peaceful.

"She doesn't have to have a reason," I said.

"This is one time I wish Ellie could see what I see." Camden put his hands in his pockets. "The very first owner was a woman named Elizabeth. She and her husband built the house back in the Thirties, and after he died, she lived here with her bulldog, Tubbs. She was cheerful, had lots of friends, gave lots of parties, and never gave up on life." He smiled. "I can see her sometimes, playing in the backyard with Tubbs. She always gives me this little salute of approval, as if she's happy I'm taking care of her home. I don't think I could live anywhere else."

"Elizabeth and Tubbs. Getting a little crowded around here."

"Oh, and get this, Randall. Her last name was Singer."

"Okay. That's too good. Ellin will just have to grin and bear it."

Bear it, maybe. Grin, doubtful.

# Chapter Eight

## *"Daddy, Let Me Lay It On You"*

That night, I had a dream about Lindsey. I was glad to see her. At first, the dreams had filled me such grief and remorse, I struggled to wake, but now that I know she's forgiven me and works with me to solve cases, I welcome the dreams. She's always dressed in her white lace dress and little white shoes, her long brown curls tied back with white ribbons. As usual, she stood at the edge of a vast misty playground. I heard other children's voices as they laughed and ran in the distance. Lindsey turned to wave at one child. Then she turned back to me, her dark eyes solemn.

*Are you going to help that girl, Daddy?*

"Yes," I said. "She might be my last case."

She seemed to waver and then became solid. *No, she's not. Other people will need your help. Don't you remember?*

"Yes, but—"

*You have to,* she said.

"There was someone else, someone who wanted justice. Do you know who that is?"

*There are lots more.*

I imagined Delores, the spirit Camden and I rescued from the mirror, sailing all over the Great Beyond, asking if any other spirits needed my services and insisting they get in touch. "Do you and Delores have them lined up over there?"

She chuckled. *Do your best, Daddy.*

I woke with a start that woke Kary, too. She rolled over closer to me. "Did you have a nightmare?"

"No. A dream about Lindsey."

She gave me her full attention. "That's good, isn't it?"

"Yes, but it's hard to live up to her expectations."

"She doesn't want you to quit, either, does she?"

"She's pretty insistent."

Kary put her arms around me. "Then you'd better do your best."

Exactly what Lindsey had said.

A sudden gust of wind sent leaves scratching at my window and whirling away into the darkness. Kary snuggled closer, and soon my thoughts whirled away into darkness, too, and I slept.

*** 

I sat at the kitchen counter Sunday morning, trying to concentrate on the lovely sight of Kary in her white bathrobe making scrambled eggs for my breakfast. Instead, I was arguing with myself about the meaning of my dream. It was pretty clear Lindsey didn't want me to quit. Something else was clear. The more Camden got involved with this serial killer, the more I wanted to find him. Not only did I want to get this creep off the streets, I wanted Camden to stop having all these hairy visions.

Not really your business, one side of me argued. It's a police matter. You haven't even been hired to find this guy. Doreen hired you to find Arliss. You need to concentrate on that. But if there's a connection to the serial killings, and I can figure it out, then I needed to try. The other people that are going to need my help—was Lindsey talking about the killer's potential victims?

"Cam seemed a little distracted last night," Kary said. "Know anything about that?"

"A woman was killed in Doreen's trailer park. Jordan hoped Camden could zero in on the murderer, so he brought over a piece of the victim's clothing."

"Doreen's trailer park? Do you think Arliss did it?"

"Camden says he didn't. Maybe we'll know more once I find

him."

"Then Cam probably saw more gross things."

"Yes, and he's annoyed because his talent doesn't work the way he wants it to. Same sad song, second verse."

She poured the eggs into the frying pan and stirred them. "Then we need to keep an eye out for illegal substances."

"I don't think he'll try pills again." She handed me a cup of coffee and I thanked her. "How did things go yesterday at the clinic?"

"It was tough at first. The smell—I guess all these clinics use the same antiseptic cleaners and have bare white walls. There were some young women there trying to act defiant, but I could tell they were scared. Most of them didn't want to talk to me, but one did. I told her what had happened to me and how she had a choice. I didn't. Would you hand me the cheese?"

I took the plastic bag of cheese from the fridge and passed it to her. "Did it help?"

She added cheese to the eggs and stirred it in. "It helped me to talk about it, and I noticed the other girls were listening even though they pretended not to. Maybe I did some good. I don't know."

For a moment, she looked so despondent, I wanted to comfort her, carry her upstairs right then, and let the eggs burn, but we were interrupted by Lottie.

"Good morning!" she chirped. "Would you read something for me?"

Kary grinned and indicated her cooking, so I took one for the team. "Sure, no problem."

Lottie handed me a large box. "Here's the fourth draft of *The Jiminy Incident*. It's all about Davidson's evil twin brother and the child he never knew he had."

"Sounds great."

"You can write any comments you like in the margins."

I opened the box and looked at the huge manuscript. It would take weeks to wade through this one. I also had a burning question about the title. "What do crickets have to do with this story?"

She goggled at me. "Crickets? Whatever do you mean?"

"Jiminy Cricket? Pinocchio? Does Davidson's evil twin have a really long nose?"

"Like the Zodiac. It's the sign of the Twins. I thought everyone knew that."

"Do you mean Gemini?"

She looked at me and then at her manuscript. She started to laugh. "Oh, my goodness. I do mean Gemini! Thank you. I don't know how that one got by me. Whatever would I do without everyone's help?"

Kary was heaping eggs on my plate. "Thanks, Kary, that's plenty."

I could tell she was trying not to laugh. "Do you want some eggs, Lottie?"

"No, thank you, dear. I'm going to work on the peanut scene. Have fun at school. Say hello to everyone for me."

She left, and Kary sat down across from me to eat her breakfast. "I think Lottie misses being at school."

I set the massive tome aside. "Could she substitute?"

"She wants to devote all her time to her writing, but I think she misses being part of a group. You've been so kind to her, David."

"Completely by accident."

She grinned. "I really appreciate it. She was my mentor my first year at Lakeside, and I'll never forget how she helped me. She was the one who taught me the Teacher Voice."

"The This Is The Last Time, Young Man, You Will Do As I Say No Nonsense Obey Or Die Voice?"

"That's the one."

"How about the Teacher Look, the intense glare that burns to the bottom of your soul?"

"Oh, I came up with that on my own."

Maybe Lottie was a better teacher than she was a writer. What could I say that would sound truthful? I was willing to do anything for Kary, even suffer through Lottie's mangled English.

For the second time that morning I said, "No problem." This time I meant it.

\*\*\*

Sunday mornings, we all went to church at Victory Holiness, a nice little all-purpose church for people who weren't concerned about skin color, gender, or financial status. Camden went because he liked to sing in the choir. I went because church was important to Kary. That is the only reason. No one wants to hear me sing.

This morning, Camden sang something about remembering, and I tried not to, but after the dream and all my soul-searching, I couldn't help but remember my past. Some days, I don't mind thinking about the perfect little nuclear family I'd once had. Unfortunately, like all things nuclear, that family went up in a cloud of smoke. Some days it bothered the hell out of me, so I'd found the simplest thing to do was ignore it and hope it went away. Foolish, of course. Useless most of the time. With Kary sitting beside me, I had other things on my mind, like our relationship and where it might go. Could I possibly construct another family, a family that wouldn't implode, or wither and fade from neglect?

When we got home from church, there was an Arliss sighting. A message on my cell phone reported that Padgett would be at Flea Pickers on I-40 just south of Parkland. I didn't recognize the voice, but figured one of Padgett's creditors was itching, you should pardon the pun, to get his hands on some of Padgett's imaginary dough.

"Ha, ha!" I said aloud. "The plot thickens."

Kary hung her coat on the hall tree. "Did your inheritance scheme work?"

"Yes, someone has decided to take advantage of the non-existent windfall."

"You want to go now or after lunch?"

"As much as I'd love to have you along, I'd better go alone. I don't want to scare Padgett off."

Kary agreed to this. "At least have something to eat first."

I took a few minutes to have some of the fried chicken and mashed potatoes that Angie had sent over, and then hitched up the faithful Fury and rode out to Flea Pickers.

\*\*\*

At Flea Pickers, a woman selling all kinds of brightly colored glass plates made a disgusted face and pointed out Arliss Padgett. The picture on his driver's license did not do him justice. The real thing far exceeded my expectations. Arliss Padgett was skinny and hunched, lank greasy hair framing a face only a mother weasel could love. I found him lurking near the drink machines that lined the fence at Flea Pickers.

"Arliss Padgett?"

Narrow furtive eyes slid my way. "Who wants to know?"

"I'm David Randall."

He groped in the folds of his dirty jacket and pulled out one of my cards, bent and smudged. "You're the man what says he has money for me?"

"That's right."

"So where is it?"

"It's in my office in Parkland. 302 Grace Street. You'll need to come by and let me see some ID, sign a few papers. That's all there is to it."

"How the hell am I suppose to know you're who you say you are? This could be a con."

Takes one to know one. "What, exactly, would I be after, Mr. Padgett?"

He had to think about that. He scowled. "Didn't know I had a rich cousin."

I shrugged. "You don't claim the money, it goes to the state. Either way, I get my cut."

A man and his wife stopped at the Coke machine and bought three cans of soda. Padgett waited until they had gone and then slid his skinny fingers into the coin return. He came up empty. "Damn."

I checked my watch. "You can spend the rest of your life scrounging for change, Mr. Padgett, or you can retire with a tidy sum, thanks to your generous cousin. It's your choice. I have other clients, other meetings." I turned to go.

"All right, all right," he said. "Where's this office of yours? I'll see if I can stop by."

I gave him directions to the house. "When can I expect you? I'm not always there."

"Later today."

"Three o'clock?"

"Yeah. Okay. Three o'clock. There'd better be something in it for me."

Oh, there'll be something for you, hot shot.

***

When I got back, Camden was waiting for me at the front door. "Jordan called. There's been another murder, and he wants me to come to the scene."

"You want to go?"

His expression said, Not really. "I promised I'd help."

"Okay," I said. "It's your psyche."

I drove him to a rundown apartment complex on the south side of town, a big featureless brick building with a sagging roof and dark windows. The neighbors clustered on one side of the yellow police tape. Jordan and two other officers stood on the other side, talking with an elderly man. Jordan waved us over.

"This is Mr. Fitzgerald. Owner of the place. He found the body."

"Not the first body I've ever found," Fitzgerald said with obvious relish.

From the looks of his place, I was surprised he ever found anybody alive.

"The victim was another blond," Jordan said. "Allison McRay. She worked in the convenience store across the street. Mr. Fitzgerald doesn't remember anything useful about the occupant, but luckily for us, another worker in the store saw Ms. McRay leave with a tall man wearing a baseball cap and a black leather jacket. This witness said Ms. McRay left willingly and assumed she knew who the man was. She didn't come in to work the next day or the next, so that's when the worker called her, didn't get an answer, and alerted Mr. Fitzgerald."

"And when I saw she was dead, I called the police," Fitzgerald said defensively. "How was I suppose to know this guy was a killer? Parsons he said his name was. Saw him only once or twice. I get lots of turnover. Nothing special about 407B."

"Didn't he give you some ID?" I asked the landlord.

"Turned out to be fake," Jordan said. "We ran it through the system and it belongs to a man who has been deceased for some time. And our killer paid for the room in cash."

"Any video of him from the store?"

"As the employee said, a tall man in a black leather jacket. The cap is pulled low so we can't see his face. But we may still be able to get something from the footage. Meanwhile, come have a look."

Jordan led the way into the dismal hallway and up a flight of dark narrow stairs. "If I had to live here, I'd kill somebody," I said to Camden. "Talk about negative vibes."

407B was the fourth door on the left. Jordan nodded to the policeman standing on guard, opened the door, and let Camden step inside.

He moved slowly into the room. It was equally dismal—faded tan wallpaper, industrial gray carpet, cheap hotel furniture, a hanging lamp like a big dead flower. The mini-fridge wheezed as if suffering an asthma attack. I'd wondered why it took three days for Fitzgerald or another tenant to become aware of the distinctive odor of a dead body. I had my answer in the overwhelming smell of mold and dust in the room.

Camden stood in the center of the room for a while. When he turned his head, I could see his eyes had changed, narrowed. He chose a particular place on the floor and sat down.

"Beautiful long hair," he said in what I called his "dead tone." "Perfect. Exactly what I need."

The other policeman started to speak. Jordan motioned for silence.

"What do you need it for?" I asked Camden.

His eyes shifted. "It's a private matter."

"You can tell me. I might know where you can get more long hair."

He held my gaze for a long cold moment. Then whatever connection he had with the murderer broke. He rubbed his eyes and came back.

"He's hiding somewhere," he said in his normal voice. "He has help."

"What kind of help?" Jordan asked.

"Someone gets him food, newspapers. He doesn't go out. He's so cautious I'm surprised he breathes for himself."

"Can you see what's going to happen next? Potential victims?"

Camden got up. He walked to the dresser and smoothed the top, as if searching for something. "The woman who was killed here, Allison. He lured her up here and then killed her because she reminded him of Margaret, a woman from his past. Margaret spurned all his advances. He hates her and loves her all at once."

"Did he kill Margaret?"

"No, but he's going to. It fills his mind, blocks almost everything else." His hands stopped and lay flat on the dresser. "He had her picture here. She's beautiful. Long blond hair, blue eyes. She looks like a model. He takes the picture everywhere. It's in a book of some kind, a book with a lot of pictures. I'm trying to see where it is."

We waited. Jordan's partner was less skeptical now, but still viewed Camden as if he might grow fangs and lunge for his neck.

"A motel," Camden said suddenly. "Crescent Square."

Jordan nodded to his partner, who was already halfway out the door.

"Anything else, Cam?"

"That's all I can get. His hatred for Margaret goes up like a wall."

"That's great, Cam, we're on it." Jordan hurried out.

I waited, but Camden didn't say anything else. "Can you see Margaret?" I asked. "She needs to know this nut is after her."

He lifted his hands. "All I can see is a beautiful blond woman and the killer's blinding hatred for her."

I didn't like the way he looked. "You all done here? I've got a dead beat dad to corral."

He gave the room one more long look. "That's all."

"Jordan," I said. "I've got Arliss Padgett coming by the house around three o'clock. Thought you might like to be there."

"I would, indeed," Jordan said.

"I'm going to have his daughter Doreen there, too."

His gaze narrowed. "You sure that's a good idea?"

"She's my client, and, unfortunately, she's still holding onto the hope he might reform. I'm afraid she's in for a sad surprise."

"Well," he said with a sigh. "She's going to have to face the truth sometime. I'll see you at three."

Camden and I got into the Fury and started for home. "What kind of book did you see?" I asked him. "A photo album?"

"I don't think so."

"This guy doesn't have a scrapbook of his victims, does he?"

"Rows and rows of pictures."

"Color pictures? Black and white?"

He took a moment to recall the image. "Some of each."

"Maybe he works in a photography studio." I stopped for a red light. "What does he need this hair for? I'm not sure I want to know."

"He's making something."

"A life-size replica of Margaret, perhaps? An altar of hair?"

"Whatever it is, it isn't good."

The light changed. I turned down Food Row and into the Dairy Queen drive-through. "Vanilla shake?"

"A large one."

A couple of slurps from a large vanilla milk shake and Camden said he felt much better.

"I'm going to pick up Doreen," I said. "Arliss Padgett's in for a little surprise today around three."

"Then I'll finish nailing down the shingles."

"You sure you feel up to it, pun intended?"

He took another drink. "Yeah, I'm good."

I dropped Camden back at the house and then drove around to the Quik-Fry.

The fast food restaurant wasn't too busy this time of day, but I had to wait behind a tired family of six who looked like they'd been on the road for weeks before I had my turn at Doreen's station.

She looked hopeful. "Hey, you got news or you just hungry?"

"Your father should be at my place by three."

Her flint eyes brightened. "I knew you'd find him. How in the world did you get him to come to your house?"

"Money talks. Let me warn you, though, he's going to be severely pissed when he finds there isn't any."

She gave a snort. "Ain't nothing new. And you ain't seen severely pissed, Mr. Randall. I'm going to give that old skunk a large piece of my mind."

"Can you get off work then?"

"Let me see." She stepped to the back and held a brief conversation with a tall gangly fellow flipping burgers. He nodded and pointed to the clock. Doreen came back, grinning. "The manager says I can have an hour, if I stay later tonight."

"I'll come pick you up."

Part two of my plan was coming together.

# Chapter Nine

### *"I Just Want a Daddy I Can Call My Own"*

Kary had gone back to the clinic, and fortunately, Lottie was writing away upstairs in her room. Just as well. I didn't think the ladies would appreciate the sight and sounds of Arliss Padgett. Speaking of sounds, I could hear the steady hammering overhead. I'd be glad when Camden finished with the roof.

I called Jordan to see if he had any news. "Any luck at Crescent Square?"

"No. How's Cam?"

"He's okay. Don't forget. I'm expecting Padgett at three."

"Oh, I'll be there. I'd like to ask him a few questions, including where was he the day Pauline Raterman was killed."

Around two thirty, I picked up Doreen, brought her back to the house, and told her to wait in the island. Not long after, Jordan drove up in an unmarked white Camry and took his place in my office. At three thirty, a clanking wreck of a pick-up pulled into the driveway. Arliss Padgett slid out. I made sure he was in the house and blocked his exit before he saw Doreen.

"Damnation!" he said. "What is this? What's she doing here?"

"She hired me to find you," I said. "Seems there's a little matter of the alimony. The rent is due."

"Rent?" he said as if I'd insulted him. "Ain't got no money."

Doreen came at him, ready to tear him to pieces. "You lousy bastard! Lazy no-good white trash! You expect Mama and me to starve? I got to work long hours at that burger place just so's we can have groceries! The court said you have to pay! What's wrong with you?"

He stepped back. "Don't go mouthin' off at me, girl. I got me a real job."

"Since when?"

"Week ago Tuesday."

"Doin' what?"

"Don't have to tell you."

"Does this mean we'll get our money?"

"Hell, yeah," he said. "You just got to be patient."

Doreen folded her arms. "I don't believe you. It's just another one of your lousy tricks."

"Tricks! You're a fine one to be talking about tricks, hiring this jerk here to lie to me, get my hopes up, and then crush 'em. You ain't much of a daughter, I'll say that."

I hated to interrupt this touching scene. "Miss Padgett, let's settle things. You want me to call the police?"

"Oh, let me call 'em," she said. "Officer Finley, would you come out, please?

When Jordan appeared, Padgett jumped as if we'd poked him with a hot iron. "We need to ask you some questions, Mr. Padgett."

He shook a finger in my face. "You lured me here under false pretenses. I ain't going with no police. I ain't done nothing."

"It's about the murder of Pauline Raterman," Jordan said.

Padgett went pale. His mouth moved, but no words came out. Then he said, "Pauline's dead?"

"I'd like for you to come with me to the station."

Padgett didn't take long to recover. His scowl darkened, the scowl of a weasel that finds the chicken he planned to eat for dinner is packing a 357 Magnum. "I didn't do nothing."

"Then you won't have anything to worry about."

Padgett glared at Doreen. "You leave me alone, girl. I want no more truck with you or that scrawny hag you call a mama. Did you set me up? Tell this cop I killed somebody? That's low, real low."

She stood, her arms still folded tight across her chest, her mouth in a firm line. Arliss Padgett cringed. What a sorry excuse for a father.

"Doreen," I said, "he's not worth it."

"I don't make enough to pay the rent." She'd been a tough little cookie up to now, but her eyes were starting to fill. The sight of Arliss Padgett live and in color was enough to make anyone cry.

"We'll think of something, right, Jordan?"

"Yes, indeed," he said. He took Arliss by the arm. "Mr. Padgett, we have a few things to discuss. Miss Padgett, I will be in touch."

She looked at Padgett and then to Jordan and back to me. No contest. "All right."

Jordan led Arliss out to the Camry. Doreen watched him go, no tears in her flint gray eyes now. "Wish to God I had me a proper daddy."

Kary's father was the founder of a mega-church in Parkland and host of the *Bible Hour*. He'd thrown her out when she got pregnant. Camden's father abandoned his mother before Camden was born. "The good ones are few and far between. Come on, I'll give you a ride back to work."

When I pulled up to the Quik-Fry, she thanked me for my trouble. "That was pretty slick, that inheritance thing. I'm not surprised he fell for it, greedy as he is."

"I don't think you should see him anymore. Leave it to the courts, one way or another. I'll help you. Jordan will help you."

She started to open the car door and hesitated. "I—I need to tell you something."

I waited while she got her emotions under control. When she spoke, her voice was still unsteady.

"When I hired you to find Padgett, I kinda lied to you. It wasn't just about the money. I was hoping if you found him and explained things and he came back and saw Mama and me that he might decide to be a good dad." She gave her eyes a swipe with the back of her hand. "It was stupid of me to think that. I see now he'll never change. I'm gonna have to take care of me and Mama."

"You've been doing the best you can, Doreen."

She pushed a strand of her hair under her Quik-Fry cap. "You said we'll think of something. Did you mean it? I can't do much more than flip burgers."

"I'll help you find a better job."

She sat in the car a few more minutes. "Can't be nothing too complicated. I'm pretty good at math, but I don't have good computer skills."

"Let's get your rent paid first, and then we'll worry about that."

She nodded and got out, turning back to ask me one more question. "Mr. Randall, do the police really think Padgett murdered Pauline?"

"He's their number one suspect right now."

She grinned wryly. "Wouldn't put it past him."

I drove around the Quik-Fry to the exit. I was ready to turn out into the traffic when I felt a peculiar swaying, as if there'd been an earth tremor. I'd experienced an earth tremor once in college when I was, believe it or not, in the library. I had quickly stepped from between the shelves. If they were going over, domino-style, I was getting out of the way. This tremor was like the one I remembered, a harmless ripple.

*So what the hell did that mean?* I thought, and that's when I heard Lindsey's urgent little voice.

*Daddy! Go home now!*

Pictures appeared in my mind like scenes in a movie. I saw Camden slip on the roof and make a grab for the gutter. I saw the gutter give way, and Camden falling over the side of the house. I whipped out into my lane, ran the light at the corner, and screeched around to Grace Street. I jumped out of the car and ran around the house. Camden was sprawled unconscious in a pile of leaves. Thank God we live near the hospital. The ambulance was there in less than three minutes.

After a few tense moments, the EMS team assured me everything appeared to be all right, but they would check him out thoroughly at the hospital. "We'll know better once we see some X-Rays," one team member told me as they lifted Camden onto a stretcher.

"Possible concussion," another team member said. He offered me a ride in the ambulance, but I said I'd follow in my car. I hurried over to Mercy General, where I filled in a thousand forms before they let me see Camden. He was still out cold, but the good news was nothing had broken loose inside.

Helps to have the skeletal density of a bird and a fat pile of leaves.

"He's going to have one hell of a headache," the doctor said. "We'd like to keep him here overnight for observation, possibly longer, depending on how he is tomorrow. Did you see what happened?"

Boy, did I ever. But no need to go into detail. "He's been repairing the roof all week. I was working in my office and I heard him go over."

"Well, he's pretty lucky. I've seen people who've fallen off ten story buildings walk away with a scratch. Others trip over a crack in the sidewalk and have brain damage. It's hard to say why some people survive."

"You have any idea when he'll wake up?"

"We'll have to wait and see. Head injuries are tricky."

I finally managed to reach Kary, and I called Rufus and Angie. You can imagine how they reacted, but at least this time, it wasn't my fault. We clustered in the waiting room, taking turns to see him, and arguing over who should stay.

Finally, I had to shut them up. "Look, this is ridiculous. Kary has to go to work in the morning, and so do the rest of you. I'll stay."

"We have to call Ellin," Kary said.

"No, we don't."

"David, she'll be upset if we don't."

"She'll be even more upset if we do. She's in the middle of some big psychic thing. By the time she gets home, he'll be okay, and he can decide if he wants to tell her or not."

Rufus stood with his huge arms folded. "If she finds out we knew and didn't call her, we won't be fit for fish bait."

"Rufus, you know how she feels about the house. The fact Camden fell off the roof while repairing it will give her all the ammunition she needs. She'll say it's too big and too dangerous. She'll have him in some sterile condo quicker than you can say one of those Southernisms you're so fond of."

"Quicker than shit through a goose?"

"Exactly."

Rufus and Angie finally saw the wisdom of this and left. Kary sat with me, her eyes filled with worry.

"Are they sure he's all right? He didn't break anything?"

"He's going to be fine."

"I wish you'd let me stay."

I wanted her to stay. "You've got to get up at six tomorrow. I promise I'll call you if there's anything you need to know."

She finally agreed. I went home, grabbed a quick bite and got a couple of books to take back with me. I hung around the room until visiting hours were over. I was about to leave when Camden opened his eyes. He looked tired and very puzzled.

"You're okay," I said. "You fell off the roof, but you're going to be fine."

"The roof?"

I figured he'd be a little foggy. "At home. You were fixing the shingles, remember?"

There was a long pause. "I don't remember."

"I'm not surprised. You took a header off the second floor."

His eyes were cloudy. "No, I mean, I don't remember anything. Who are you? Where am I?"

This did not sound good. I pulled my chair closer. "My name's Randall. David Randall. You're in the hospital. You were up on the roof at home, and you must have slipped. You tried to grab the gutter, but it gave way and you fell."

He started to move his head, winced, and didn't try again. I could tell none of this was getting through. "I'll get the doctor."

A short while later, a couple of doctors came by and said that with concussions, patients often experienced temporary amnesia.

Ellin was due to arrive in four days. "It had better be temporary."

"Just give him time," one doctor said. "Time and plenty of rest. We'll see how he feels tomorrow."

# Chapter Ten

*"Papa, Mama's All Alone Blues"*

Monday morning, Camden was much better. He remembered his name and mine, had to take a moment before he remembered Kary's name, and was still fuzzy about the details of his accident. The doctor wanted to keep him in the hospital one more day.

On my way out of the hospital my cell phone rang. It was Jordan, his voice concerned.

"I heard Cam fell off the roof. Is he all right?"

"He was lucky to fall into a big pile of leaves. He'll be okay, but he's kind of out of it today."

"Damn. We could use his help."

I stopped in my tracks. "Don't tell me there's been another murder."

"No, but we had a break at Crescent Square. Our surveillance team caught a tall man wearing a black jacket and a baseball cap."

"Wow, you guys are good. Case closed."

"Not exactly. His name's Franklin, and the manager of the motel hired him to haul off some metal canisters. We checked him out, and he's not our guy. But he told us he was approached by a man his height who gave him the jacket and the cap in exchange for his black hoodie. Said the man seemed nervous."

"I'll bet he was. Did you get a better description?"

"A couple of pieces to the puzzle. Franklin said he spoke in a clipped voice and had long thin hands. I was hoping to bring the jacket and cap by your house and let Cam have a go at them."

"That won't work today. He's still in the hospital and barely remembers his own name."

"Damn," Jordan said again. "How about you?"

"I remember my name."

Jordan gave an exasperated snort. "I mean, can you come over and have a look? You know the kind of things Cam looks for, and you might see something we're missing."

Jordan had to be desperate to ask for my help. I drove over to the Crescent Square Motel where Jordan stood at the front door. The walls of the motel were cracked and dirty. Plastic bags had drifted and shredded against the chain link fence that surrounded the parking lot. I expected a welcoming party of rats and cockroaches to greet me.

"We've got to stop meeting like this," I told him. "Where do you want me to look?"

"Around back. That's where Franklin said the man approached him." The back of the Crescent Square Motel was just as appealing as the front. A long row of metal canisters stood rusting in the sun beside an ancient Dumpster. Camden probably could've touched them and had a revelation, but I did not want to touch them and knew it wouldn't do any good if I did.

"Did Franklin notice anything else about the man? Maybe his eyes or his hair color?"

"He said when the man took off his baseball cap he was bald."

"Maybe he's gathering hair to make a toupee." I looked at the wads of candy wrappers and empty packs of cigarettes, wondering why the manager didn't hire this Franklin to pick up all the trash. "Where was the motel manager when this clothing exchange happened?"

"Manager's out of town."

If I had to look after this dump, I'd be out of town, too, as often as possible.

Jordan rubbed the bridge of his nose. "I've got everybody I can spare working on this case. Several suspects have come up in the database, so we're checking them all. This man's got a hideout somewhere."

"Anything on Margaret?"

Jordan sighed. "Do you know how many Margarets live in Parkland? Plus the one he's after could live anywhere around here. Madison, Celosia, Windy Grove. I've got some people on it, but it's a long shot. Still, we've got more info than we had before. When do you think Cam will be well enough to handle the clothes?"

"I'll let you know," I said. "He should be home by tomorrow."

***

As much as I hated the thought of dealing with Arliss Padgett anymore, I kept remembering what Camden had said. *I have a feeling something really bad is going to happen, and Arliss is part of it.* The really bad something had happened, and poor Pauline Raterman was dead, but what if Arliss was involved with other bad somethings? Doreen had decided she didn't want to see him again. But I had a feeling of my own that my time and trouble with Arliss wasn't over.

I spent most of my morning calling around and looking online to see if there were any jobs available for Doreen. Around lunchtime, Jordan called to let me know his officers had found a black hoodie in a pile of clothes outside a Goodwill. "Franklin identified the hoodie as his. So our killer has changed clothes again, more than likely taking something out of the Goodwill bag."

"No surveillance cameras at the Goodwill?"

"Not around the corner from the usual drop off location. We're back where we started."

"What about Arliss?" I asked. "Did he have anything useful to say about Pauline Raterman?"

"No, but we're holding him on contempt of court charges, which is what happens if you don't pay your alimony, as you are no doubt aware. I let Miss Padgett know."

"Thanks." I was glad to hear that at least for the moment Arliss was off the streets. After a quick sandwich, I headed back to the hospital. Camden was asleep, and Lottie sat by the bed, writing away in her notebook.

"Hello, David," she whispered. "The doctor was just here. Everything's fine."

I pulled up another chair. "Thanks for staying."

"It's no trouble. I've gotten some wonderful ideas. What do you think about this for the title of Randolph and Preston's next mystery? *Diagnosis Murder.*"

"That was a TV show with Dick Van Dyke."

"Oh, that's right. I'd forgotten." She looked down at her notebook. "What about *Operation Murder?*"

"Sounds like a war movie."

She frowned as she erased her notes. "Well, it will come to me. Titles are sometimes the hardest to come up with." She brushed the paper off. "Kary tells me you found that young girl's father."

Last night, I had filled Kary in on the Last Deadbeat Dad. "Yes, and I'm all done with him."

"So what's your next case?"

Technically, I wasn't on the serial killer case. "I've got a few things lined up."

"It must be very exciting."

Only if things go as planned, I wanted to tell her. Which they rarely do.

***

Tuesday morning the doctor said Camden could go home but to make sure he got plenty of rest. At the house, we parked him in the island for our convenience. Kary took a day off from school, and she and Lottie made a nest for him on the green sofa and agreed to take turns watching him. For most of the morning Camden lay there like a little worn out sock.

I was getting myself a cola in the kitchen when Angie came in carrying a paper sack. She put the sack on the counter and called round the corner to Camden.

"It's Angie, remember? You doing okay?"

He must have nodded or said something, because she came back to the kitchen. "Has he been all right today?" she asked me.

"Sleeping mostly."

"I'm worried about him, Randall. He doesn't look good."

"He's tougher than he looks."

She took a carton of ice cream from the grocery sack. "See if he'll eat some of this."

I got a spoon out of the drawer and took the carton to the island. Camden was awake, but just barely. Angie was right. He didn't look good. He looked like a kid who'd badly misjudged the length of the monkey bars at school.

"Want some of this?"

He nodded. Kary helped him sit up and arranged the pillows behind him. The slight color he usually has was back in his face.

She handed him the carton. "Fudge Vanilla Swirl," she said. "It's on your top ten list."

"Thanks." His eyes were cloudy. I couldn't tell if this was from all the sleep or the bump on the head. He ate slowly, uncertain, like someone who's just discovered what a spoon is for.

"How do you feel?" I asked.

He touched the bandage on his forehead. "This hurts a little. Not bad. I can't think very clearly, though."

"Anything come back to you about the accident?"

He ate another spoonful of ice cream. "I remember waking up in the hospital. I remember Angie giving me some water. And Kary. At least, I think it was Kary." He paused to rub his eyes wearily. "A lot of different faces. I can't put names to them yet."

"You will. Don't worry about it."

"I keep having the strangest dreams, even when I'm awake. I keep seeing accidents and fires and stuff like that." His eyes were large with worry. "This is even more weird. Sometimes, it's as if I can hear what people are thinking."

Over the sofa, I exchanged a glance with Angie that asked the same question. Do we tell him? Not now, I decided with a shake of my head. It might be too much.

"Must be the medicine," I said. "Everything will come back to you."

Kary gave me the same questioning glance and reached for the empty glass on the coffee table. "You need some more tea, don't you?"

"Yes, thanks." He waited until Kary was in the kitchen and then said, "Lots of things are coming back, but these day dreams are driving me crazy. What did they give me in the hospital?"

Okay, so maybe this was the time to explain. "Actually, you're probably seeing the future. You're clairvoyant."

I expected several reactions, but not this one. He laughed. "You're kidding!"

"Nope. In fact, you're a very accurate clairvoyant. You can take somebody's hand or an object and tell all sorts of things. Past things. Future things. If you get really riled, you can move stuff around just by looking at it."

I let this sink in. "Is that what I do for a living?"

"No, you don't like doing it. You're always telling me you want to live a normal life."

He took a long moment to consider this. "Do I live a normal life?"

"Usually. This is the first time you've fallen off the roof."

He winced. "I remembered that today. My foot slipped, and when I tried to grab hold of the gutter, it broke off. I thought I'd fixed those gutters." His eyes held mine intently. "But this clairvoyance—if I'm so good, why didn't I see that coming and get down before it happened?"

"You've always told me you don't see your own future, or if you do, it's hard to interpret."

"Well, that's damn inconvenient, isn't it?"

Kary came back with the glass full of tea. "Here you go."

"I hope you remember Kary," I said.

"Yes, of course, I do." He closed his eyes for a moment and then opened them. "I keep seeing a little girl. Long brown curls, white dress."

"That's Lindsey. My daughter. We have her to thank for the warning."

"I see three other children, but I think those are mine. That's hard to believe."

"They're not here yet. Hope you remember you're married."

"Ellie." Just my luck he'd remember her. "She was here a while ago."

"Huh? You must have dreamed that part." No way Ellin would have let me off the hook so calmly. I turned to Kary. "Has Ellin come home?"

"No, she won't be back until Thursday, remember?" Kary took the wedding portrait off the piano and brought it over.

I showed it to Camden. "This is Ellin. For God's sake remember that. Otherwise, no power on earth will be able to save us."

He looked at the picture, and to my relief, smiled in that sappy way he smiles when he sees his wife. "Of course I remember her."

"Don't ever forget. She's going to be mad enough if she finds out about this accident of yours."

"Someone really should call her," Kary said.

"No, no," I said. "Camden will be fine by the time she gets back. No need to alarm her."

There was a knock on the front door. "I'll get it," I said. To my surprise, there was Doreen Padgett in her orange and white uniform of the Quik-Fry team, her saddlebag on her hip and her hair tied back in an untidy ponytail.

She invited herself in, along with the smell of French fries and onions. She saw Camden and stopped. "Gosh, what happened to you?"

"He fell off the roof," I said.

"Wow. No kidding?" She came into the island and sat down by Camden, her sharp features softening. "Hey, you doin' all right?"

"You'll have to tell him who you are," I said. "He's still confused."

She spared me a quick glance full of concern; then spoke to Camden. "I'm Doreen. Doreen Padgett. Randall's solved a case for me." She turned back to me. "My mama says to thank you for helping us out. She didn't think much of you at first, but now she says if you're willing to help me find a better job, she figures you're all right. Says she'll talk to you about what she seen the other day when Pauline was killed."

"Didn't she tell the police everything?"

"She don't like them. Says she'll talk to you, if you'll come by."

"All right, I will. Do you need a ride back to the Quik-Fry?"

"I got some time before my next shift."

"How about I give you a ride home, and I can talk to your mother?"

Doreen agreed to this, told Camden to take care, and followed me out to the Fury.

She opened the passenger side door. "Now this is a fine old car."

"Gets me where I want to go."

Doreen slid into the front seat. "That real pretty girl in there. She Cam's girlfriend?"

"No, she's my girlfriend. She's more like his sister."

"I never seen anybody so pretty. Is she a model?"

"She teaches second grade."

"I'd be a model if I was that pretty." She grinned. "Cross that off your list of jobs."

I tried to be tactful. "Any woman can be a model."

We drove down Food Row and passed the Quik-Fry. "I hate that old place," Doreen said. "I'll be glad to see the back of it."

"Don't quit yet."

She turned that intense flinty gaze toward me. "Oh, I know you'll find something. You have the talent, Randall, that's for damn sure. Look what a short time it took for you to find Padgett."

I shrugged. "I got lucky."

"It's more than that. I'll bet there's lots more people who could use your help."

It was as if I heard Lindsey's words echoing in Doreen's rough little voice.

*Other people will need your help. There are lots more.*

Doreen averted her gaze. "Don't mean to tell you your business, but that's how I feel about it. If you're good at something, you stick to it."

If I knew how I felt about it, maybe I could stick to it, I wanted to tell her, but I didn't know, so I said, "That's okay."

\*\*\*

The trailer park was just as dismal as I remembered. Hazel Padgett met us at the door to her trailer and stood back to let me enter. I didn't think it wouldn't be too pleasant inside. I was surprised to find that despite the cheap paneling, saggy chairs, and cracked linoleum, everything was scrubbed and clean. Even so, the trailer smelled musty and old. Doreen disappeared down a short hallway. Hazel Padgett offered me a seat.

"No, thanks," I said. "You had something to tell me?"

She nodded, her arms hitched up under her chest. "Told the police I didn't see nothing, but that ain't quite true. Told 'em I come out to check on my laundry. You see, I snuck out to meet somebody."

"Pauline?"

She snorted. "Not Pauline! A man."

"A man?" Not the killer. Surely not that.

"Well, hell. Arliss ain't been around forever, and when he is here, he's good for nothing. I got needs, same as anybody."

"Who were you meeting, Mrs. Padgett?"

She looked behind her to make sure Doreen wasn't listening and lowered her voice. "Married man, but unhappy, you know what I mean? Like, his wife, she don't understand him? Doreen don't know, and don't you tell her, neither. Wouldn't be good if this got out."

"I understand," I said, even though my imagination wasn't up to the challenge. "So when you went out to meet this man, you saw something besides Pauline's body?"

"Yeah, I seen another man creeping around. Kinda tall and skinny, with long fingers. Didn't recognize him. Don't know why he was there. Didn't make sense. Anyhow, he bolted when he saw me, and that's when I saw Pauline."

"Can you remember anything else? What he was wearing? Did he have a car? Did he go into another trailer?"

She screwed up her features in thought. "I was right surprised, expecting to see Tyrone and him being out there instead. He had on a white shirt and brown pants. Didn't have much hair himself, as I recall. I heard a car start up, but didn't see it."

"Do you think Tyrone saw anything?"

"I don't know. Never did see Tyrone. Guess he couldn't get away."

Doreen returned. Her mother gave me a wild look, as if she expected me to tell Doreen about her aborted rendezvous of passion with the lucky Tyrone.

"That's very helpful, Mrs. Padgett, thank you," I said, and she relaxed. "Anything else you think of, please call me."

"What'd you tell him, Mama?" Doreen asked.

"That's between him and me, girl."

Doreen stood just like her mother, her arms folded under her non-existent breasts. For a moment, I knew exactly how Hazel must have looked at eighteen. "I'm the one what hired him."

"You let him do his job and leave me alone."

I did not want to get in the middle of this argument. "Doreen, you need a ride back to work?"

"That'd be nice, thanks."

"You're not worried about staying here, are you?" I asked as we got into the Fury. "You and your mother could come stay at Camden's a few days."

"We're all right," she said. "The whole place was spooked about Pauline, but we're looking out for each other now. We'll lock up good. The best thing is knowing Padgett won't be back. Oh, and I need to thank you for having your policeman friend take care of Padgett. He called me and said they was holding him on account of being in contempt of court. 'Course that don't mean he'll pay, but I still appreciate the effort."

I'd forgotten to ask her about the rent money. "Will you have enough money for this month?"

"They'll let me slide for a few more weeks. By then, you'll have me a new job, right?"

"Right."

She smiled briefly, and I could see how young Arliss might have been attracted to young Hazel. "I'm counting on you, Randall. I know you'll do your best."

*Do your best, Daddy.*

Now I really had to.

# Chapter Eleven

## *"I'm a Long Gone Daddy"*

**B**ack at home, Camden was asleep. Kary sat in her chair, reading from her laptop, a textbook titled *Intro to Clinical Counseling Methods* propped beside her chair. She glanced up. "Did Doreen's mother have anything useful to say?"

I plopped down in the blue armchair. "She went out for a secret tryst with the local trailer park stud and saw a tall, skinny bald man with long fingers. She said he had on a white shirt and brown trousers and ran away when he saw her."

Kary found a piece of paper to mark her place and shut her book. "First of all, ten points for 'tryst,' and second, is Doreen's mother the kind of woman who would have them?"

"No. I would have to call Rufus for a proper description. Anyway, Lover Boy didn't show. She told the police she went outside to check on her laundry because she didn't want to mention this rendezvous."

"Any idea why the killer targeted that woman in Doreen's neighborhood?"

"Not a clue."

Kary set the stack of papers on the coffee table. "Well, while you were gone, Cam tried to convince me he wasn't psychic. After he went to sleep, I called the doctor to see if he could explain what was going on. He said that sometimes a head injury could cause selective amnesia."

"Selective amnesia, like 'I don't want to remember I'm psychic'?"

"Yes. If I were further along in my studies, I could probably tell you more about the underlying psychological reasons, but I think we know what those are."

"Too bad Slim and Jim Python aren't here to set him straight." A surprise visit from the large friendly snakes had taken care of Camden's drug problem. "Maybe it's time we got our own."

Kary gave a little shudder. "No, thanks. The doctor said in most cases, the patient eventually recovers all his memories whether he likes them or not."

"Let's hope by eventually he meant four days. Did you find any Padgetts at your school?"

"Oh, yes, I almost forgot." She reached into the book bag propped against her chair, pulled out her cell phone, and checked her notes. "There are the Padgett twins, Letty and Freddy, Tempest Padgett, Armand Padgett, and Epiphany Padgett. None of them are related to Doreen's family. I talked with Armand's mother, and she said she knew who Arliss was and was forever grateful her Padgett family tree did not branch that far."

"Epiphany Padgett. Now there's a name for one of Lottie's characters."

Kary closed her lap top. "What else can I do? What are your plans to catch this serial killer?"

Kary hated when I tried to shield her from danger, but damn it, the man was after blonds. "I'm leaving that to Jordan."

"But you caught Arliss, so you have a little free time here."

"No one's paying me to track down the killer." I realized as I said this, my last case had been solved. I'd found Arliss Padgett. True, he hadn't paid what he owed Hazel, but I was finished. I was free. Free to do what?

"That hasn't stopped you before."

I was thinking so hard about my sudden freedom, Kary's words didn't register. "What?"

"Not having a client hasn't stopped you before. Are you okay?"

"I caught Arliss Padgett, and he isn't the killer, so I guess I'm done."

She stared at me for a long time. "We talked about this. You weren't going to give up."

"I don't see it as giving up, exactly, I—"

Kary gave me one of her best Teacher Looks. This was the one that said, "Enough nonsense, young man." "Cam has decided he isn't psychic, and you've decided you're not a detective. But guess what? You don't have the excuse of falling off a roof. You are giving up because you're feeling sorry for yourself, and trust me, I know what that feels like." I tried to cut in, but she steamed on. "How about this? I'll hire you to find the serial killer. We need to get him off the streets and out of Cam's head, and you're the man for the job." She held out her hand. "Deal?"

I knew when I was beaten. I shook her hand. "Deal."

"I'll expect daily updates."

"Yes, ma'am."

"Also the friends and family discount."

"You got it."

Her stern look softened. "You know this is what Lindsey would want."

I knew exactly.

"Good," she said. "Now all we have to do is convince Cam that he is indeed psychic."

***

By the time I hauled myself out of bed Wednesday morning, it was almost ten o'clock. Camden was up and around, navigating the kitchen. He'd put on a sweatshirt and jeans. He didn't look quite as frail.

I yawned as I wandered toward the coffee maker. "Looks like you're feeling better."

"I think I remember where everything is." He took a glass down from the cabinet, poured some tea into it, and sat down at the counter.

I got a mug from the counter. "Name, age, serial number?"

"Camden, thirty, work at Tamara's Boutique."

"Yup."

He took a drink of tea, grimaced, and added more sugar. "That's all I can manage right now."

"There's one other little detail."

"The psychic thing. What's the deal about long blond hair?"

"You're helping the police track down a serial killer. All the victims have had long blond hair."

He gave me a large stare. "I'm not ready for this."

Then he probably wasn't ready for this, either. "Jordan Finley has some clothes he'd like you to hold."

"Good Lord. I'm supposed to get some—what?—some vibes from these clothes that will lead them to the murderer?"

"That's usually how it works."

He put the glass of tea down. "I need something stronger than tea for this."

"Nope. You can't drink alcohol. It makes you crazy."

"Oh, like I'm not crazy now? My life is coming back in bits and pieces, only the pieces are things I'd rather forget."

I brought my coffee to the counter. "It'll all come back. You fell off the roof, for God's sake, what do you expect?"

"So am I always helping Jordan on these cases?"

"No, this is a special occasion."

"A special occasion."

"You don't like to throw your psychic weight around because usually no one believes you."

He paused. "Am I that accurate?"

"Yes."

He thought about this for another long moment. "Anything I need to know about today?"

"You're going to relax and enjoy a bad science fiction movie. *Phantom Planet* is on channel eighty-seven."

Before we could start the movie, we had visitors from Victory Holiness, three church ladies, bearing food. The first one in the door was Mimosa Simmons, a tiny black woman who played the piano for the services.

"Cam, honey, how you feeling?" She set a huge casserole dish on the table. "The Jessie May Carter Circle sent you some dinner."

She was followed by two other little women loaded down with

dishes, baskets, and pans. One heaved a fat apple pie onto the table. "We were most distressed to hear about your accident. What were you doing up on the roof, anyway?"

"Trying to fix some shingles," Camden said. "My goodness, you really didn't have to go to all this trouble."

"No trouble at all." The other woman put a pan of rolls next to the largest casserole dish. Everything smelled wonderful. "You just rest and get well. You've got a lot of singing to do in the next few days."

Fortunately, Camden remembered he could sing. "I hope to be back very soon."

Mimosa patted his cheek. "Don't rush things. You're looking kinda peaked." She pointed out some of the dishes. "Now, Millie Carter sent some of her brown sugar pound cake 'cause she knows that's your favorite, and Tammy Louise sent her special green beans and ham 'cause she knew Randall here would help you eat those, and this is Beulah's chicken casserole that you don't have to eat if you don't want to, but we didn't want to hurt her feelings. Pastor Mark says he'll stop by later on. He says he saw you in the hospital, but you don't remember, and you just call me if you need anything else."

"Thanks very much," Camden said. "Won't you stay and have some of this?"

The ladies were already heading out. "My, no, that's all yours," Mimosa said. "You get well now. We'll see you in church."

Camden and I looked at the huge pile of food. I picked up a roll. "Ready for a snack?"

"I believe I could eat something."

We had made our way through the macaroni and cheese when we heard a car drive up. I went to investigate. Jordan got out of his unmarked car. He looked as if he hadn't gotten much sleep, either.

"Ready for an early lunch?" I asked him. "Meals on Wheels was just here."

He came in and walked around the table, admiring the food. "Quite a spread. I'll have one of those rolls if you can spare it."

"Help yourself," Camden said.

Jordan sat down and reached over for a roll and the butter.

"You feeling all right?"

"Pretty good," he said. "I've still got a few holes in my memory, but the important stuff has come back."

I sat down at my seat and resumed feasting. "Except for the clairvoyance. He doesn't believe he has it."

"It's a little weird," Camden said.

Jordan munched his roll. "You must not want to believe you have it. You've never liked it, so you're blocking it out." At my look of amused skepticism, he added, "We cops have to know something about psychology. Think of the nutballs we run into every day."

"That's deep, Finley, very deep."

"Thank you." He took a paper bag out of his pocket. "Now you don't have to do this if you're not up to it, Cam."

"I don't remember how to do this," Camden said.

"Just give it a try."

Camden took the baseball cap out of the bag and held it cautiously, as if it might burst into flames. "No," he said after a while. "I'm sorry. Nothing."

"You're sure?" Jordan took the cap back and handed Camden another bag. This one was filled with several long strands of blond hair. "Try this."

"More hair?" I said. "What the hell is he doing with it, stuffing a mattress?"

"Forensics took these off the jacket," Jordan said.

Camden opened the bag and carefully felt the hair. He shuddered. "This is really gross."

"Anything?"

He shook his head. "I'm sorry. I don't know what I'm supposed to see."

I glanced at him, curious. I had the feeling he was not telling us the whole truth. "You'd know if there was anything there."

Camden went to the sink to wash his hands. Jordan put that bag away and reached for another roll. "It's okay, Cam. We'll try again when you're back to normal. Trouble is, we're no farther along than we were. Apparently, Mr. Clairol's gone underground."

I reached for the green beans. "Mr. Clairol?"

"That's what the newspaper's calling him now. I'm sure he loves all the free publicity, but I don't. This is just the kind of thing that sends Parkland citizens into a tailspin. Oh, and get this, Randall. Technically we couldn't keep Arliss any longer, and we were all set to let him go when he got into a fight with one of the officers."

I couldn't imagine Arliss Padgett summoning enough courage to punch a policeman. His wife and daughter, yes, but not a large armed policeman. "A fight? Arliss?"

"Damnedest thing. Hauled off and socked Porter in the eye, then tried to grab his gun." He shrugged. "Happens sometimes."

"So you've still got him?"

"Yes, indeed."

At least this way he wouldn't be beating up on Doreen and her mother. "Keep him as long as you can."

"That's the plan." He got up. "See you later, Cam. Take care of yourself."

"I will, thanks."

I walked out with Jordan and we stood on the porch. "Arliss seemed a bit disturbed about the murder," I said. "Are you sure he doesn't know anything about it?"

"Not only is Arliss a disturbed individual, he is deeply stupid. My best guess is he doesn't know anything." He opened a new pack of cigarettes, took one out and lit it. He blew a puff of smoke. "Cam thinks that fall knocked all the psychic out of him, but he saw something when he touched the hair."

"Yep. He's not fooling anybody."

"I don't suppose there's much we can do about it until he decides to be helpful." He blew another stream of smoke. "Guess now that you found Mr. Padgett, you're on the lookout for your next deadbeat dad."

"I haven't caught this serial killer for you yet."

Jordan gave me a look. "I know I let you in on what we know so far, but you really ought to stay out of this."

"Now that Camden's gone normal, I'm your best bet."

"I don't think so."

"Kary thinks so. She hired me."

"Even if that were true, which I doubt, it doesn't change my mind."

"I spoke with Doreen's mother yesterday. She gave me a description of the man: tall, skinny, long fingers, bald, dark trousers, white shirt. Matches what you learned from Franklin and other witnesses."

He gave me a long considering look. He took another puff of his cigarette. "Anything else?"

"I'll share anything I find."

He and I both knew sharing important information wasn't always the case. "All right," he said. "You're in. But on a very limited basis. I don't want you poking around, scaring this guy off."

Lottie came out to put an envelope in the mailbox. "David, where did all that food come—" She went wide-eyed at the sight of Jordan.

"Jordan, this is one of Camden's tenants, Lottie Lee McAllister," I said. "Lottie, Jordan Finley of the Parkland Police Department. Homicide division," I added, just to set her off.

Lottie's eyes bulged further. "Oh! Oh, my gosh! Could I use you as a reference source? I know a little about police work, but to have a real policeman as a consultant would add so much to my work!"

"Your work?"

"I write mysteries, what the British call crime novels."

"We call them something else around here," I said.

Lottie chattered on while Jordan maintained the calm listening expression he uses with all suspects. "You see, I have several detectives. There's Dick and Dora. They're very rich, and they have the cutest dog that helps them solve crimes. There's Timothy Mullins, who's blind, but his other senses are extra-heightened. There's Chief Windfeather, who calls on the spirits of his ancestors. Oh, and there's Mrs. Gillyflower. She only seems to be scatter-brained, but really, she has a razor-sharp mind. She lives in the little seacoast town of Billing's Crossing and knows everyone and everything."

"That sounds very interesting," Jordan said.

"Oh, and mustn't leave out Randolph and Preston. I think they must be my very favorites. Davidson Randolph is tall, dark, and handsome, and his very best friend, Preston, is small, blond, and so cute you just want to pick him up and hug him."

Jordan turned his sudden snort of laughter into a sneeze. "Excuse me."

"Officer Finley—or do I call you Chief Inspector or something?"

"Detective Inspector," he said, enjoying himself.

"Would you consider reading one of their adventures and telling me what needs to be corrected?"

"I'd love to."

Lottie beamed. "I'll go get their latest escapade."

She dashed back into the house. Jordan turned to me. "Randolph and Preston?"

"Has to be read to be believed."

Lottie bounced back out. "Here we are! I can't tell you how excited I am at this opportunity." She handed Jordan a pile of paper. "This is the sixth draft of *Death and the Dreamer*. In this one, Preston has all sorts of premonitions—he's psychic, you know—and his dreams lead Davidson Randolph to the real killer."

"Really?" Jordan said. "That's very original."

"You see, the killer has this huge casino, but it's actually a front for his money laundering and drug running. His lucky number is five, so he calls himself Big Five. He shakes down everybody in Vegas."

"Sounds like a tough guy."

"Oh, my, yes. He's a member of the Coasta Rico."

Jordan turned this chuckle into a cough. "Oh?"

"He's also a wise guy in the Mafia. You wouldn't want to tangle with Big Five."

"Could I take this with me? My fellow officers might have some suggestions."

Lottie was delighted. "That would be splendid, thanks! David, I'm going to go put all that food away. We don't want anyone to get salmineo."

"I think she meant salmonella," I said, as Lottie went inside. "English is her second language, possibly her third."

Jordan was still chuckling. "Where did Cam find that one?"

"She's one of Kary's friends."

He hefted the manuscript. "Well, I can't wait to read this. Keep in touch, Randolph."

# Chapter Twelve

*"Mean Daddy Blues"*

Jordan drove off, and I went back inside. There was no sign of Lottie so I assumed she had dashed back upstairs. Camden was asleep on the sofa, our gray cat, Cindy, curled on his chest. I crossed the foyer to my office where I found Lottie sitting in the client chair.

"Oh, hello," I said. "Can I do something for you?"

"David, I don't want you to think I'm prying into your affairs, but I can't help overhearing what's going on. You're hunting a serial killer, and I know all about them."

I sat down at my desk, prepared to politely listen to the latest Randolph and Preston adventure, thank her for the information, and return to my real work. "You do?"

"Yes, in many cases, the serial killer was abandoned by his mother and lives with a horrible fear of rejection, so in order to avoid it he kills people before they can reject him. But it's really very difficult to determine the serial killer's motivation. Is your suspect act-focused or process-focused?"

Okay, was not expecting that. I'm sure my expression said, "What?" because Lottie explained.

"The act-focused killer kills quickly while the process-focused killer kills slowly."

"I believe he is act-focused."

"Visionary or missionary? Does he hear voices that tell him

what to do, or does he believe he's on a mission to rid the world of a certain ethnic group, or the elderly, or something like that?"

"He's targeting blonds because a blond rejected him in high school."

She nodded, satisfied. "There you go. Fear of rejection, act-focused, and missionary. Although, a killer can have many motives, and his motives can change over time. He could be acting out of enjoyment, a need for power or thrills, anger—the list goes on."

I was impressed. "Lottie, this could be very useful, thanks."

"Well, I did say I wanted to help. It's easy to find whatever you need on the Internet. I did tons of research when I was writing *The Many Murders of Meadowbrook*. I'll have to let you read that one."

"You've saved me a lot of time," I said. "Thank you."

She hopped up. "You're welcome. Now I must get back to work." She hurried out and went up the stairs. I turned to my laptop to do my own research when I saw Doreen come up the walk carrying an orange and white Quik-Fry bag.

I met her at the door.

"Hey," she said. "Thought I'd bring you guys some cheeseburgers."

"Did you walk all the way from the Quik-Fry again?"

She shrugged. "I didn't mind. I got some time and wanted to get out of there."

"Come in. Camden should be awake by now." I was full of church food, but took a cheeseburger to be polite. Doreen tiptoed into the living room. Camden was awake, refilling his tea glass from the pitcher on the coffee table.

"Oh, hi, Doreen."

"Brought you a cheeseburger."

I knew he was stuffed, too, but he thanked her, unwrapped the burger, and took a bite. "Delicious. That was very thoughtful of you."

She blushed and sat down in the chair beside the sofa. "Well, I didn't think you'd feel like cooking." She smoothed her hands on her orange and white slacks. "It's my break, so I thought I'd drop by and see how you were doing."

"I'm fine, thanks." He leaned back on the sofa, and Cindy settled herself in his lap, angling for a bite of burger. "You mind if I share this with Cindy?"

"No, she's sweet."

"Her kitten's around here somewhere," Camden said. "His name's Oreo."

"He's in my office," I said. "Why don't I give him some of my cheeseburger?" Why don't I give him all of my cheeseburger, I decided. I went back to the office. Oreo had been in and out all day. I found him in my trashcan. He was glad to take care of the burger. When I tuned back in on the island conversation, Doreen was singing her same sad tune.

"Wish to God I had me a proper daddy. What's yours like, Cam? Bet you don't have such a sorry case as Arliss Padgett. Bet yours is cute like you."

"To tell you the truth, I don't know if he's sorry or not," Camden said. "I've never met him."

"Oh," she said. "Oh, sorry, I didn't mean nothing by that."

"It's okay. I've only recently connected with my birth mother. I spent my younger years in foster homes."

"That's too bad, but can't be no worse than what I've got. You don't know nothing about him?"

"Not a thing."

"What about your mama?"

"Her name is Denise. She lives in Richmond and has a whole new family."

"You going to visit?"

"She's been here a couple of times."

I could tell Doreen found this hard to believe. "Just a couple? She don't know how nice you are, or she'd want you to visit more. How'd you know about her?"

"Randall found her for me."

"He's good."

"Yes, he is."

Ah, unsolicited testimonials. Yeah, I was great at finding things. Keeping them found, now, that was the tricky part.

"So get him to find your daddy," Doreen said.

"I don't think so."

"Why not? Ain't you curious what he's like?"

He paused, and I wondered what he'd tell her. "I'm afraid of what Randall might find."

I thought Doreen might press the issue, but she showed some tact and changed the subject. "Randall's gonna see if he can find me a better job. Not too much out there if you haven't finished high school."

"I know," Camden said.

From her dramatic pause, I could tell she was staring at him. "You didn't finish high school, neither?"

"No, I dropped out when I was sixteen. Now I wish I'd finished. Maybe someday I'll go back."

"But look at all these books laying around," she said. "You read a lot, don't you? I can't read too good, but I'm a whiz at math. I can add up numbers faster than a calculator. That's why I do good at Quik-Fry."

"I'm sure Randall can find something better for you."

"Well, I'd better go. Hope you get well soon."

Doreen paused at my office door. "I gotta get back to work. Call me when you know about another job."

I offered her a ride, but she said she'd rather walk. She hadn't been gone ten minutes when Rufus came by with a pizza.

"Hey, Cam," he said, "how many possums does it take to have safe sex?"

"I had no idea possums practiced safe sex," Camden said.

"Well, the answer's three. Two to do it, and one to direct traffic." He roared with laughter and set the large pizza box on the coffee table. "Brought you a snack."

I usually can't say no to pizza, but I was full up to my neck with church food. "Just what we need, Rufus. More food."

"Yeah, but you ain't got this new Dieter's Rebellion." He sat down in the blue arm chair and opened the box to reveal a giant pie overloaded with pepperoni and sausage. "You want some, Cam?"

"Thanks, but the church ladies brought a ton of lunch, and Doreen stopped by with cheeseburgers."

"Okay, then." He pried a piece loose and stuffed it in his mouth. When he could talk, he said, "You feeling okay?"

"Pretty good."

"So Doreen was just here, was she? How's she doing, Randall? What's the latest on that scuzzbucket she calls Dad?"

"He's in jail for hitting a policeman."

He gave a snort. "Sounds like something he'd do. If brains were dynamite, he wouldn't have enough to blow his nose."

"I told Doreen I'd help her find a better job. You know of anything?"

Rufus untangled a long string of cheese from his beard. "Can't see her working construction. Maybe Angie knows something. I'll ask her."

"Thanks." I went back to my office mainly to avoid the smell of pizza and the sight of Rufus eating it. I had phone calls to make, my continued job search for Doreen. I called the Drug Palace and asked Ted if he needed another sales clerk. He didn't have any openings. I checked with Bilby Foster at his pawnshop, but he'd just hired his cousin to help in the store. Mandy at the public library promised to let me know if there were any job openings.

I sat for a while, pondering my next move. Now that Jordan had given me the okay on the serial killer case, I could check with some of my other sources. Maybe one of them had heard something about Mr. Clairol.

Rufus had gotten to the punch line of another joke. "And then the little old woman says, 'Well, whatever it is, it sure needs ironing.'"

I came back to the island. One piece of pizza sat in the box.

"Saved you one," Rufus said.

"No, thanks." I turned to Camden. "I'm going to ask around about Mr. Clairol. Want to come along?"

His expression was wary. "I don't know how I could help."

"You could help by picking up some useful vibes."

"I don't think I can do that."

Rufus gave him a scowl. "Of course you can. You do it all the time."

"Not anymore."

"Well, hell, I don't think you can get rid of it."

"Whatever it was, it's gone."

"I need to slap some sense into you?"

"No."

Rufus started to say something else, caught my eye, and then shrugged. "Okay." He picked up the pizza box. "I'll leave this last piece in the kitchen in case somebody wants it. See you later."

Camden busied himself with the *UFO Monthly*. I tried one more time.

"I could really use your help."

He kept his eyes on the magazine. "I'm not psychic anymore."

"Maybe you don't want to be, but you still are, and you know it."

He didn't say anything else, so I left without him.

# Chapter Thirteen

*"Poutin' Papa"*

I stopped in at Janice's, Talley's, the Elms, Bilby's pawnshop, and places where in the past I'd gotten some good leads and clues for my other cases. This time, I came up dry. If Camden had been with me, I might have had better luck, but I had to admit I couldn't always rely on the signals he picked up from handshakes, or the visions certain objects might produce. But it was frustrating as hell to think he might have helped me catch this guy when all he was doing was sitting at home feeling sorry for himself and giving Lottie more ideas for her cockeyed mystery novels.

I drove out to the trailer park in the hopes of talking with some of the neighbors. The place looked deserted, and the few inhabitants I could coax from their TVs to their front doors didn't know anything. One fellow came to the door with a shotgun in one hand and a Mountain Dew in the other.

"If I catch anybody snooping around my trailer, I'll shoot 'em," he said.

"Have you seen any strange people, or maybe a strange car you didn't recognize?"

"Seen a Honda in here one time with the roof tore off. I think that was somebody's idea of a do-it-yourself convertible."

"Did Pauline Raterman have any visitors lately?"

"She's got a passleload of cousins always messin' around, but I ain't seen none of them, not since she died, anyway."

I thanked the man for his trouble and made a mental note to ask Rufus how many people made a passleload. In the Fury, I called Kary and gave her a rundown of my day's activities. "Not much luck, so far."

"At least you're working on it."

"Yeah, well, a certain someone made it clear I'd better."

"I'll bet you've stopped feeling sorry for yourself."

"You're right. I've been too busy to mope."

I could hear the smile in her voice. "Told you so."

\*\*\*

When I returned to 302 Grace, my luck really ran out. Ellin had come home early. Fortunately, Camden was awake and fairly conscious. They were hugging and kissing as if she'd been gone for years. Ellin is a beautiful woman with golden curls and big blue eyes. She's Camden's height, five seven, and looks every inch the successful career woman. Just don't get on her wrong side. It involves a lot of pain and cringing, like biting into a piece of aluminum foil.

She pushed Camden's hair back to feel his forehead. "Are you okay? You look tired. Not getting the flu, are you?"

"I'm fine," he said. "How was your trip?"

"Wonderful. We got some great footage for the show. Come help me unpack the car and we'll decide about Saturday. I'm so excited about the reunion."

We were both lucky she was so excited. For one thing, it had her in an unusually good mood. For another, she didn't notice Camden's slight memory lapses. We got all her suitcases in and hauled them upstairs to their bedroom. When we got back to the island, she went to the bookshelf and pulled out her Parkland Senior High School yearbook.

"I know it's only a fifteen-year reunion, but I can't wait to see some of my old classmates. A lot of them moved away, but practically everyone is coming, so it will be fun to catch up."

"And see if they match their Facebook pictures?" I said.

For once, she enjoyed my joke. "Oh, definitely." She found the page she wanted. "Look at this if you want a really good laugh."

Actually, the high school version of Ellin was a pleasant picture, her hair longer and her smile sweeter. She was not yet the fierce control freak we all knew and feared.

"Look, Cam, this is Jamie Conners from the bank. Can you believe it? And here's Roger Ames. Oh, and I wanted to show you how fat Patricia Prentiss was."

Pictures.

Hadn't Camden said something about rows of pictures?

I glanced over her shoulder and to my surprise saw a familiar face on the P page. "Was Arliss Padgett in your class?"

She grimaced. "Unfortunately, yes."

Arliss at eighteen was a skinned weasel, awkward and wary in his ill-fitting white shirt and dark tie, lank hair hanging in his eyes.

"Friend of yours?" Ellin asked.

"Father of a client. I thought he was much older."

"He's your client's father? Must be the child he had when he was sixteen. That caused a lot of talk around school, believe me." She turned a few more pages. "Cam, here's Stanley Wainsettler. You remember me telling you about the time he blew up the science lab?"

I saw Camden stiffen as he looked at the row of faces on the W page. From his puzzled expression, I knew something had popped into his mind, and he either didn't know how to interpret it or didn't want to. I glanced at the faces, unable to sense anything. Everyone looked pretty much the same. The girls had approximately the same hairstyle, blouses, and jewelry, and the boys looked uncomfortable in their shirts and ties. There were a couple of skinny guys who could've grown into Mr. Clairol. Ellin chatted on about Stanley, a fat cross-eyed fellow in the middle of the row. Stanley might have been a fat teenager, but many plump teens lost weight and lost their hair. Any one of these smiling boys could've been twisted inside.

Camden sat back as if disturbed by what he'd seen.

Ellin looked up from the yearbook. "What's the matter?"

"Headache."

"I really think you are coming down with something. I'll get you some aspirin."

As soon as she left, I picked up the yearbook. "What did you see?"

"I'm not sure," he said. "There was a feeling of intense hatred. I don't understand."

"On this page? Can you tell which picture caused that feeling?"

"I'm not touching that book."

"Okay. Tell me which picture."

He wouldn't look at the yearbook. "It's gone."

"Camden," I said, irritated. I heard Ellin returning from the downstairs bathroom.

He shook his head. "I don't like this. All these things in my head. I can't sort them out. Just leave me alone."

Oblivious to our exchange, Ellin leaned over the sofa and handed Camden two aspirin. She went around to the kitchen to get a glass of water and came back looking puzzled "What's with all the food in the kitchen?"

"Leftovers," I said, hoping she wouldn't press for details. Explaining about the church ladies would only lead to why they had showered us with food. "Ellin, anybody in your class named Margaret?"

She picked up the yearbook and thumbed through the pages. "Margaret Layton. Homecoming queen, head cheerleader, and all-around airhead."

A vague-looking blond smiled up from the page. Could this be Mr. Clairol's Margaret? "Any idea where she is now?"

"I know she'll be at the reunion. She'll want to bask in all the old admiration. Everybody thought she was hot stuff. With any luck, she'll be fat and wheezing."

I took the yearbook and turned back to the W page. "Anybody on this page who was crazy about her?"

"All the boys lusted after her, and all the girls were jealous as hell. Typical high school behavior. Why do you want to know?"

"Just curious."

She took back the yearbook, closed it, and put it on the coffee table. "Cam, I want to go by the studio and check on everything. Do you feel like coming with me?"

"I'll stay here, if that's all right."

She gave him a long critical look. Usually she'll remind him of their extremely complicated arrangement of monthly studio visits he agreed to, but he obviously wasn't feeling well. "That's probably a good idea. I won't be long."

When she'd gone, I gave Camden a long critical look of my own. "You can stop using your accident as an excuse."

He gave me a glare Ellin would have envied. "And what excuse are you using?"

"We're not talking about me and my not so mid-life crisis here. We're talking about you helping find a serial killer. Use your powers for good. Isn't that what you're always saying?"

"I don't have any powers."

"Fine. Be a regular jerk."

"You need to leave me alone."

"Or what? You'll magically toss stuff around the room? Come on, try it. I've seen you do it." Could I get him angry enough?

His eyes were not quite the blazing hot blue that preceded a full-on telekinetic burst. "What are you talking about?"

"You're telekinetic, too. Didn't I mention that?"

The pitcher full of tea began to shake, along with the *TV Guide*, the yearbook, and a few cat toys under the coffee table. Camden glanced at the objects in alarm and sat back on the sofa. The objects settled.

"Looks like powers to me," I said.

His voice was unsteady. "I'm not going to do this."

"Okay," I said. "When you decide you want to be useful, let me know."

*** 

If Camden wouldn't help, then maybe Arliss would. When I swung by the jailhouse for a chat with Daddy Dearest, I took Ellin's yearbook with me. Jordan let me use one of the interrogation rooms, brought Arliss in, sat him down, and stood behind him.

Arliss Padgett scowled when he saw me. "You happy now?"

"Delirious."

"Well, you and Doreen ain't gettin' any money. Can't even pay to get myself out of here."

"You're fine right where you are, and since you've got nothing else to do, how about answering a few questions?"

He turned away. "Ain't doin' nothin' for you."

"The policeman standing behind you is a personal friend of mine. If you cooperate, I might be able to help you."

He turned back, a light in his weasel eyes. "Yeah? So what kind of questions?"

"Did you go to Parkland High School?"

This set him off balance. "Whadda you take me for? I went to high school."

"Parkland High School?"

Another weasel glare and a sullen reply. "Hoorah for the blue and white, go, Bears, go."

"Do you recall a girl named Margaret? Real pretty, blond, blue eyes, the model type?"

He squinted up his little eyes to give that massive brain more room to cogitate. "Don't know."

"I brought along something to jar your memory." As I turned the yearbook pages, Arliss gave a running commentary on his former classmates.

"Stuck up, damn phony, shithead, stuck up, pansy, jock, grease ball, stuck up— oh, that's her."

The pretty vacant-eyed blond Ellin had ID'ed. Margaret Layton Douglas.

"Stuck up." That seemed to be Padgett's all-purpose remark for any woman who didn't go for his nature-boy charm.

"Was there anyone who hung around Margaret, anyone she might have laughed at, given the cold shoulder?" Besides you, I wanted to add.

"Don't recall," he said. "Don't care. Bunch of high and mighty fatheads. Too good to have anything to do with me."

"So it's not likely you'll be attending the class reunion on Saturday."

He gave me what I'm sure he thought was a manly smirk. "Shows what you know, smartass. I done sent in that RSVP thing.

I want to see what all those jerks look like now."

"Really? Well, I hope you have a good time." I turned to the W page, the page that had given Camden a shock. "What can you tell me about the people on this page?"

He glanced at the page and grimaced. "Don't remember half those losers."

"It's entirely possible one of these boys killed Pauline Raterman." I didn't miss the second glance he gave the page. "Maybe when he was in high school, he was into drugs and violent video games, or liked to draw pictures of people getting killed, or had a mama who smacked him all the time." Damn, I could be describing Arliss.

Arliss eyed me suspiciously. "Why're you asking me all these questions?"

"I want to catch this serial killer."

"Well, I ain't helping you."

"You'd rather be charged with Pauline Raterman's murder?"

"They ain't got enough to hold me."

"Then why did you hit a policeman? Looks to me like you want to stay in jail."

He hunched a shoulder and didn't answer.

"You do, don't you?" I said. "Why? What are you afraid of?"

"Nothin,'" he said. "Get out."

I closed the yearbook. "If the police don't have enough to keep you, sooner or later, you'll be out, and if you're in league with this killer, he's going to think you talked, and even if you're the farthest thing from blond in Parkland, he'll come after you. A little something for you to mull over."

"You don't know a damn thing," he said.

I did know at least one damn thing. I knew that somebody on the right hand side of page W in Ellin's yearbook had Arliss Padgett good and spooked. I'd seen the way his eyes darted to that side of the page, the same page Camden refused to look at again. So I had a starting point.

Jordan took Arliss back to his cell and then we sat down in Jordan's office. Jordan sat back in his swivel chair. Around him, the police station hummed with activity, phones ringing, computer keys clicking, criminals whining. He took another look at Margaret Layton Douglas' yearbook picture. "So this might be the Margaret everyone's looking for. What about the other page you showed him?"

I turned to the W page. "Camden had a reaction to this page."

"Anyone specific?"

"He's still insisting he's not psychic, so no."

Jordan counted the pictures. "We know the killer's a white man, so I count twenty out of thirty-five possible suspects here. This is where you bow out, Randall."

Oh, he wasn't getting away with that. "Are you kidding? You wouldn't be this far without me."

"You wouldn't be this far if Cam hadn't seen something."

"Camden's useless right now."

Jordan put a large finger in the yearbook to hold his place. "Useless, maybe, but also safe at home. I'm going to make a copy of this page. Then *you're* going to go home."

Nothing I said convinced him I'd be helpful. He copied both W pages and returned the yearbook to me. Then he jerked his thumb toward the door.

"Out."

***

I went by the Quik-Fry to tell Doreen the good news and the bad news. She was delighted that Arliss was still in jail and disappointed about her job opportunities.

"It's like I told Cam, I can't do much of anything," she said, "but I thank you for trying."

"Don't give up yet. Something'll turn up."

I drove home and found a strange car parked out front. A client? No such luck. Garrett Henderson, my thick headed stalker, glowered from the porch. He smelled as if he'd been swimming in beer.

"I've come to kick your sorry ass," he declared.

"Thanks, but it's already been kicked today," I said. "You want to leave? I'll give you a running start."

Henderson growled and bounded down the steps. I still had the yearbook in hand, so I clouted him over the head. The first blow didn't make as much of an impact as I'd hoped, but the second one did. He rolled over and landed in a soggy heap on the lawn.

"You've got five minutes to clear out before I call the cops," I said.

He muttered something that sounded like, "I don't have to."

"No, here's what you have to do. You have to get up, dry out, and start being responsible. If I ever see you around here again, I'll really give you something to whine about."

He staggered to his feet, gave me an evil glare, and went on his way.

# Chapter Fourteen

*"More Time Papa"*

Henderson was long gone by the time Ellin got home from the PSN studio which was one good thing that happened today. I was in my office and heard her go up the stairs. Jordan had his twenty yearbook suspects, but I still had the book, so I did, too, and I didn't recall him saying I was banned from using the Internet. I eliminated the girls, African Americans, Latinos, and Asians from page W and started looking up the leftovers. I located eighteen of the twenty former Parkland High School students. One was in Alaska, five were overseas serving in different branches of the military, four had passed away, and one was a priest in New Jersey. Seven still lived in Parkland. Of these seven, one worked for the local Rotary Club, and his picture on their website showed a round jovial red-haired man. One was involved with Greenpeace and was off on a ship somewhere saving whales. His picture showed a grim, determined bearded man. The remaining five men, a chubby banker, a very short grocery store manager, a lawyer with impressive facial hair, a tattooed florist, and a bulked up truck driver, did not fit the profile. There was no information on two of the twenty, Joshua Westfield or Bradley Wallace. As teens, both men had nondescript features and brown hair. According to the yearbook, Westfield had been captain of the Debate Team and editor of the school newspaper. Wallace had played basketball.

Ellin came to my door and stood, arms crossed. "Randall, did you involve Cam in one of your stupid cases while I was gone?"

I put on my best and most innocent expression. "Why do you say that?"

"He's just acting a little—I don't know—the way he gets when the two of you are up to something."

"Ellin, I promise you, he is not involved with my current and only case."

"What exactly is your current case?"

"I'm trying to find a job for a young woman named Doreen who wants to better herself. Any openings at the PSN?"

My distraction was successful. "There will be, if Reg doesn't get his act together. I can leave for one day, and he makes a mess. You can imagine the chaos he created while I was gone for a week."

I didn't have to say, "Tell me about it." She poured forth all of Reg's crimes, including his revamping of the sacred schedule and all the weird people he'd booked for the PSN shows. Apparently Reg was not familiar with Ellin's Scale of Weirdness.

"Now he's started telling Bonnie and Teresa what to wear. I suppose he fancies himself some fashion guru." She paused. "You got me off the subject."

"What subject?"

"Involving Cam in your cases."

"I told you I haven't."

"He doesn't look like he feels well."

Well, when you have a headache *and* a guilty conscience, I suppose you don't.

She spied the yearbook open on my desk. "What are you doing with my yearbook?"

I was lucky the impact on Pumpkin Man hadn't left any dents. "I thought I recognized someone." I pointed to the W page. "What can you tell me about Joshua Westfield and Bradley Wallace?"

She picked up the book for a closer look. "Bradley played on the basketball team. That's all I remember about him, and Josh actually didn't graduate with us."

"Why not?"

"His mother was from Ireland, and he decided to go live with her. I remember we were all sorry to see him go. He was a nice guy."

"He has a Parkland address."

"That's probably his father. His name is Joshua, too."

That narrowed it down to Bradley Wallace.

"How would you know either of them?" Ellin asked. "You didn't move to Parkland until you were in college, right?"

"They just looked familiar," I said, hoping she wouldn't press for more details.

Fortunately for me, Ellin thought of something else. "And, really, what's with the massive amount of food? It looks like one of those covered dish suppers they're always having at Cam's church."

I couldn't have asked for a better opening. "That's exactly what it was. It was our turn to bring home the leftovers."

She accepted this, and I congratulated myself on an excellent save.

I hunted for Bradley Wallace without success until Kary came in from school.

She set her book bag on the hall tree and accepted the Diet Coke I handed her. "David, have you told Ellin about Cam's accident?"

"No. I value my life too much."

"My goodness, can't she tell something's wrong?"

When Ellin is caught up in her job, she's not observant, and she lacks the usual woman's intuition that my two ex-wives always used to their advantage. "He distracted her with a headache."

"Where are they now?"

"Ellin's upstairs unpacking and Camden's taking a nap. Please don't say anything yet. Camden will tell her if he wants her to know."

"I don't like lying to her."

"You don't have to lie. She's not going to ask you if he fell off the roof, is she?"

At the sight of the dining room table loaded with food, Kary stopped. "My goodness, what's all this?"

"Church food, delivered by Mimosa and company. The rest is in the fridge. The macaroni and cheese is really good."

Kary broke off a piece of pound cake. "How did you explain

this?"

"Leftovers from a covered dish supper."

"You are such a good liar. But Ellin will have all our heads when she finds out."

"If she finds out. Let me change the subject. Are there any job openings at your school? Teacher's helpers, or whatever they're called. I'm trying to find Doreen a better job."

"She'd have to have a teacher's certificate."

"Even if she's cafeteria worker? She's used to working with food."

"I don't think there are any specific requirements. I'll check on that." She finished her piece of cake and wiped her hands on one of the paper napkins the church ladies had provided. "Update, please."

"I have something interesting."

We went into my office. I opened the yearbook and I showed her the picture of young Arliss.

"Poor fellow didn't improve with age, did he?" Kary said.

I realized that if Arliss was in Ellin's class, he was in his thirties and a father, like me. The contrast couldn't have been more pronounced.

I turned the pages. "Ellin wanted Camden to see a fellow on the W page. I know he saw something else, something disturbing, but he won't admit it. Arliss had a similar reaction when I showed him the same page. I've narrowed it down to this guy, Bradley Wallace. All Ellin could tell me about him was he played on the basketball team." I turned back a few pages. "Here's Margaret."

"She's blond, all right."

"Homecoming Queen, cheerleader, not the kind of girl to give Arliss or Bradley a second glance, I would think."

"So how do we find Bradley?"

"I thought I'd stop by Parkland High tomorrow. Some of the teachers might remember him."

"I have an idea."

I braced myself. Telling her no would only make her more determined.

"Speaking of remembering, if Bradley Wallace went to Parkland High School, there's a very good chance he came up through the Parkland school system. Why don't I see if some of the elementary teachers remember him? Maybe they'd have more insight into his character, or even know where he might be living now."

"That's a great idea," I said, relieved that her plan didn't involve sneaking around dangerous areas of town in disguise.

"Not only that, but Lottie can help me. She has thirty years experience in the schools and knows practically everybody. She can ask all kinds of questions and no one will suspect a thing."

"You're right about that."

I closed the yearbook and set it aside. "You know, actually, as my client, you are not required to help with the investigation."

"Nope, don't give me that. As your client, I call the shots."

"And you're the best client I ever had."

"Flattery will not help you," she said with a grin. "We have a serial killer to catch."

\*\*\*

I wasn't sure if Camden sensed he was in trouble or if he really needed to sleep. In any event, he didn't come back downstairs that evening. Ellin came down briefly to get something to eat. Then she went back upstairs. Lottie filled her plate with green beans and ham and a chunk of apple pie, chattering excitedly over being a part of the investigation.

"You know I will do everything I can to help. I thought I'd start with Parkland Elementary and work my way up. I know lots of people, and someone's bound to have a clue. I'm ready to go through every grade."

"I've got the high school covered," I said.

"Then I'll take care of all the rest." She turned to Kary, who was sitting at the counter doing her guidance counselor homework. "My goodness, Kary. Every time I see you, you're reading that huge textbook. When will you be through?"

"Not for a very long time," Kary said. "I can afford only one or two classes a semester, and after I get a Bachelor's, I have to get a Master's degree in guidance."

"Well, I admire your determination."

Lottie went upstairs to work on her master plan. I spent another hour at the computer with no luck. When I came out to the island, Kary was sitting in her rocking chair crocheting. Kary liked to crochet little multicolored squares and fashion them into afghans. She was making an afghan for one of her teacher friends who loved bright colors, so the squares piled on the coffee table were red, blue, and yellow. She must have had enough studying because she was working on another square.

She turned the little square to finish the last side. "Did you find out anything else about Wallace?"

I sank down in the blue arm chair. "No, and my eyes are crossed from staring at the computer screen."

She put the finished square on the stack. "Mine are tired of reading. I'm going to do a few more squares and go to bed."

"Want some company?"

"That would be very nice."

One of the balls of red yarn had escaped the basket. I scooped it up, pulled a long thread, and started making loops on the coffee table.

She peered at my effort. "What are you doing?"

"Writing 'Marry me.'"

"Your cursive needs work."

"Give me the scissors."

"No, you're not going to cut up my yarn."

I rolled the yarn back into a ball and tossed it to her. "Let's finish this conversation upstairs."

Later that night as I watched Kary sleep, I held her close and smoothed her silky hair. As much as I worried about her reckless streak, I had to admire her spirit. Speaking of spirits, I hadn't heard from Lindsey in a while. Maybe I'd dream of her tonight.

# Chapter Fifteen

*"Tree Top Tall Papa"*

I didn't have any dreams that night, not even a hint. Did this have anything to do with Camden's reluctance to accept his clairvoyance? He had a direct line to Lindsey, too.

I was brooding about this over my morning coffee when Lottie dashed in to grab an apple from the bowl on the counter.

"I'm on the case!" she said as she hurried out.

Kary was next in the kitchen. "Running a little late this morning," she said. She took her lunch bag from the fridge, gave me a quick kiss, and was gone. Then Ellin came in to fill her coffee thermos.

"Randall, I called Tamara and told her Camden needed another day or two at home. He needs to let this cold run its course."

I'd hoped Camden would tell Ellin about his accident. That would be the easiest way to diffuse the situation, but he was letting everything slide. He had to know the longer this went on, the more spectacular the explosion.

Ellin gave me her best narrow-eyed stare. "You're sure he's not helping you with some bizarre case."

"He's not doing a thing to help me," I said, which was the truth.

\*\*\*

Parkland High School was a huge brick building crouched behind ancient trees. It had the cheerless presence of most educational institutions built in the Thirties, a gloomy façade that not even the blue and white "Go Bears!" banner could disguise. In the front hall was a large display case filled with trophies and photos. It was easy to find the ones from the year Ellin graduated. The basketball team had won everything there was to win. The team nickname had been "The Dynamite Bears." Although most of the photos listed the team members' names, Bradley Wallace in his senior year looked like every other tall, gangly white boy. He and another boy, Thad Able, had been co-captains. There was one constant in all the photos, however. Coach Mac Stevens looked the same, heavyset and beaming.

The school secretary informed me that Coach Stevens was still on the faculty. She called his office, and he agreed to speak with me. I walked down to the gym where he greeted me at his office door. He was a little grayer and a little heavier, but still smiling.

"I've got a few minutes before my next class, Mr. Randall. What can I do for you?"

I didn't want to tell the coach that one of his star players might be a serial killer, especially with only Hazel Padgett's description to go on. "I'm writing a book about championship basketball teams, and I was hoping you could give me a little information about the Dynamite Bears."

"Sure, sure. Come in."

Stevens' office was jam-packed with more trophies and photos. I sat down across from a surprisingly neat desk. Stevens wedged himself behind the desk. "One of the best teams I ever coached," he said. "You know, sometimes everything comes together. Those boys worked like they had one mind. Plus they were all good students. I never had any trouble with any of them."

"Did any of them go pro? Able, perhaps, or Wallace? I noticed they were co-captains."

"Thad Able played for Duke while he was there, but he wasn't quite good enough for the draft. Wallace, I don't know. I don't hear from a lot of the boys once they leave."

"You know how I can reach Able?" I asked, thinking the

co-captains might still be in touch. "I'd like to interview him for the book."

"Yeah, he's in Chapel Hill. Get a card from him every Christmas."

Coach Stevens found Able's phone number and address and wrote them down for me. Then before his next class arrived, Stevens told me all about the Dynamite Bears and their many successes. I thanked him and told him I'd send him a copy of my book if I ever finished it.

*Maybe I should let Lottie write it for me*, I thought as I went back to the Fury, and on the way to Perkie's Coffee Shop, entertained myself imagining the title she'd choose. *Dribbled to Death* was my favorite.

*** 

At Perkie's, I got a large cup of coffee, and sat down in a quiet corner to call Thad Able. After explaining about my book and my recent talk with Coach Stevens, I asked him about his high school experiences with the Dynamite Bears and his friendship with Bradley Wallace. Able rambled on about his victories and then described Wallace as a quiet fellow who'd been very single-minded about basketball.

"Bradley could be pretty intense," he said. "His home life wasn't the best, so he really threw himself into sports."

I recalled Lottie's information and the fact that many serial killers were abandoned by their mothers. "When you say his home life wasn't the best, did he ever tell you anything about it?"

"He never went into detail, but I think he was about six when his mom left."

"Left? Abandoned him?"

"I guess. He never said why."

"I'd like to interview him for the book, too. Do you ever see him or talk to him? Friends on Facebook?"

"We used to email. Then he got married and after about a year, he and his wife split up. His wife was a looker, let me tell you. I didn't think Bradley could attract a woman like that." He chuckled.

"Well, he could attract one, but he couldn't keep her, apparently."

"Blond?"

"Yeah. How'd you know?"

"It's always a blond, isn't it?" I said and he chuckled again. "That's the last you heard from him?"

"Guess the last time we spoke was about a month ago."

"So you have a current email address? Phone number? Home address?"

He dug out his phone. "I don't have his email, but I think I still have his number. Hang on." He searched his contacts. "Yeah, here it is. Let me call him right now. He'd be interested in being in a book about the team." He punched in the number.

I waited, thinking it can't be this easy.

It wasn't.

"Dang," Able said. "No longer in service. Sorry about that."

"That's okay," I said. "Do you know where he's living now, or what he was doing?"

"The only address I ever knew was Lancaster Mills, but he's not there anymore. When he was married, he and his wife lived in Summer Lakes until the divorce. She moved out of state, and I think he's somewhere in Asheville. He never talked about himself. Mainly he wanted to talk about the Bears, what the team was like this season, how Coach was."

"Anyone else on the team who might be in touch with him?"

"Bradley kept to himself, mostly. I mean, when we were on the court, the whole team was in sync, you know? But afterwards, he'd head on home. He was pretty serious about his studies. We hung out some, but not a lot."

It suddenly occurred to me that Bradley Wallace might come to the reunion.

"So he's not the kind of person who'd come to your senior class reunion?"

"Oddly enough, during our last conversation he said he might come to see some of his old team mates."

To see Margaret. To lure her to a dark place and peel her head. Good God. What if that was his plan? If Bradley Wallace was Mr. Clairol, and if he had the nerve to show up, was it possible I could catch him at the reunion?

"Kind of surprised me because he never was one for parties," Thad Able said. "I hate to miss it, but my daughter's birthday is the same night."

"Anyone else he'd come to see? Margaret Layton, maybe?"

"Margaret Layton. Well, I hadn't thought of her in a long time. No, Bradley wouldn't care about that. She was so far out of his league. Out of my league, too. Unless she's changed a lot, she probably won't be at the reunion. Not classy enough for her. But you might meet Bradley there."

"Thanks." That's exactly what I plan to do. "And thanks for sharing your experiences as a Dynamite Bear. I'll let you know when the book comes out."

"Those were some great years," he said. "Maybe the best years of my life."

It didn't sound as if those years had been Bradley Wallace's best.

\*\*\*

I slid into the Fury and reported my findings to Jordan.

"Another dead end," I said. "I had high hopes for that phone number."

"But Able gave us a couple of starting points. I'll check with the police department in Asheville and have someone check out the Summer Lakes connection and possibly find Mrs. Wallace. Our killer's bound to make a mistake sooner or later," he said. "Keep me posted."

I was wondering how Ellin would feel about me attending her high school reunion when Kary called.

"Ready to report," she said.

"That was fast."

"Lottie put the word out on the grapevine, and we have a lead on Wallace's mother. We think she lives in the Lancaster Mills neighborhood."

The neighborhood Thad Able had mentioned as Wallace's childhood home. "Not the best neighborhood."

"Oh, but we will be in disguise."

I knew it. "Just remember you are very blond."

"No one will recognize us, trust me. And I have a request. Books And More called, and the book I ordered for Ellin's birthday is in. Would you possibly have time to go by and pick it up? I have a teachers meeting this afternoon, and then Lottie and I are going to Lancaster Mills."

So was I. "Not a problem."

As promised, I stopped at Books And More in Friendly Shopping Center. The shop had books and more, as advertised. I wandered through displays of stuffed animals, cookies, designer coffees, and gift-wrap to get to the counter.

"I'm here to pick up an order for Kary Ingram," I said to the salesgirl.

She searched behind the counter and pulled out the latest romantic thriller by Ellin's favorite author. "Here it is."

"Could you gift wrap that, please?"

"Yes, sir. We have flowers, hearts, blue foil, or silver."

"Flowers will be fine." Something caught my eye, a row of white mugs decorated with quotes from different books, including one from Sherlock Holmes. "I want to buy one of those mugs, too. You can wrap it in the heart paper."

While she wrapped the gifts, I thought I'd see what else I could find in Books And More. Mistake number one was pausing at the children's section. There on the end cap was a complete collection of the *Little House* books, Lindsey's favorites. I'd never seen the appeal of them, myself, but I'd read her every single one, getting the Wilder family through the long winter and onto the prairie and over to the banks of Plum Creek. I turned away to see *My Father's Dragon* gleaming from another shelf. Lindsey had loved those books, too, all three adventures featuring a smart little boy named Elmer and his friend, a blue and yellow striped dragon.

Damn.

I moved on to the jewelry section. Mistake number two. Dangling from a plastic rack were delicate little gold lockets, each one engraved with a different initial. Of course the one with the "L" was prominently displayed. Lindsey had loved her gold locket, changing the picture inside every week. One week it was her best friend's picture, one week it was the teddy bear's picture—where was that locket? I guess Barbara had it. Suddenly, I wanted it. I wanted it more than anything.

*You're doing it again, Daddy. Don't be sad.*

My heart skipped a beat. Lindsey.

*Sorry*, I thought back. *Didn't mean to wallow.*

*Are you helping that girl?*

*Yes, I'm doing all I can to find Doreen a job. I'm sure something will come up.*

*The other girl.*

*Other? Was that who called me on my car radio, the one who wanted justice?*

"Sir?"

I could tell from the salesgirl's expression this wasn't the first time she'd tried to get my attention.

"Sir, your gifts are ready."

I came back to the counter and paid for the mug. The book was perfectly wrapped in the flower paper with a white bow. The mug had been put in a box and the box wrapped in pink and red heart paper with a pink bow and little red streamers. "They look great. Thank you."

"Was there something else I could help you with today?"

You can tell me who the other girl is because I have no idea. All the way home, I tried to contact Lindsey, but I didn't hear anything else from her.

# Chapter Sixteen

## *"My Daddy Rocks Me"*

I thought Lottie would still be out interrogating her former co-workers, but I found her at home seated at the dining room table, her laptop open, and several notebooks around her.

She glanced up, beaming. "Good news, David. You might recall I sent *The Raging Rapids* to Voltage Press? Well, they've agreed to publish it."

I didn't recall that, but I was happy for her. "That's great news."

"Voltage has some very good deals, and I get to design my own covers."

"So you're going to self-publish?"

"Yes, I've decided that's the best way to go." She gathered up the notebooks. "I'm still working on the case, though, don't worry. Kary and I are hoping to find Bradley Wallace's mother this afternoon."

"Yes, she told me. That's great news, too." I looked around. "Where's Camden?"

"He's fixing something out back."

I set the presents down on the dining room table and walked to the back bay window. Fixing something out back. I hoped Camden wasn't up on the roof again. He was reattaching one of the rockers on a rocking chair. At first, I thought it was one of the porch rockers, but this chair was smaller and in much nicer condition. I went out for a closer look.

"What are you working on?"

"Rufus found this in his garage. I thought Ellie might like it."

"Nice. I guess you heard Lottie's good news."

He carefully hammered a nail into the rocker. "She was bouncing off the walls earlier. I'm glad she decided to give Voltage a try."

"Does she have enough money stashed away to pay for several hundred copies of *The Raging Rapids*? Although, one copy would be one too many."

He set the chair right side up and gave it a test rock. "The way she explained it to me, she can pay for as many or as few as she likes."

I gestured toward the chair. "You think Ellin will get the hint?"

"Hint?"

"Rock-a-bye baby?"

"I'm pretty sure we'll have children some day."

"Three of them." When he gave me a skeptical look, I added, "You told me so yourself. You saw three children in Ellin's future, so let's hope they're all yours."

"I wouldn't mind having three children, but I don't think that's something anyone can predict."

"Okay, fine," I said. "Continue to live in denial."

He put his tools back into his toolbox. "Would you mind getting the chair?"

Camden brought his toolbox, and I carried the chair inside. Lottie had left the dining room for parts unknown. I set the chair in the island and then went to the fridge to make inroads in the church food. There was plenty of macaroni and cheese left, as well as an assortment of sandwiches and veggies.

"Let me change the subject," I said. "I'm planning to go along with you to Ellin's high school reunion."

Camden put his toolbox in the kitchen closet. "Why? I have to go, but you don't."

"I want to be there when the serial killer strikes."

"What are you talking about?"

I took my full plate and sat down at the counter. "Arliss Padgett had the same reaction you did to that page in Ellin's yearbook. I talked to the coach at the high school and the fellow who was co-captain of the basketball team Ellin's senior year. I have a strong suspicion that the killer is Bradley Wallace, a quiet serious guy who didn't go to parties, whose family life sucked, and who's been through a bad relationship with a beautiful blond."

"All that doesn't make him a killer."

"No, but your reaction to his picture is a good clue. I'm hoping Wallace will be at the reunion, make a stupid move, and I'll catch him."

Camden got a Coke out of the fridge. "You just said he was a quiet guy who didn't go to parties."

"Not unless there's a chance he can get to Margaret Layton, his dream girl."

"You're welcome to come along, but it doesn't seem likely anything will happen."

"You say that now, but wait till you get there and start picking up signals."

He sat down on another stool and sighed. "Randall, I'm not picking up signals."

I stopped eating and put a hand to my ear. "What's that? I hear the Land of Denial calling."

"I'm feeling much better today, but I'm not having any sort of visions or premonitions or whatever."

"If you say so."

The pattering of feet on the stairs announced the return of Lottie. She burst into the kitchen.

"David! Cam! Wonderful news! I've had an apostrophe!"

I looked around for a newborn punctuation mark. "Sounds painful."

She laughed. "Oh, lord, I meant epiphany! The most wonderful breakthrough! I now know exactly how to get Davidson Randolph and Preston out of the tiger trap!"

"You should have asked me," I said. "Whenever I'm stuck in a deep hole with a smaller person, I boost them up and out and they return with a rope."

"My goodness, that's so trite! You see, Randolph will take some of the broken spikes and rub them together until they start to smoke."

I grinned at Camden. "So you get charbroiled Preston."

"No, he uses his jacket to create smoke signals to let the maharajah know where they are. The Raj is out tiger-hunting, so he'll be in the neighborhood."

"Wouldn't it be a lot simpler to boost Preston up and let him go for help?"

"It would, but Preston has had a relapse of his old drug addiction problem and is reliving the terrible car crash that claimed his parents."

"That must be entertaining."

Lottie was absent from school the day they taught Irony. "Oh, no, it's dreadfully sad. The poor dear needs immediate medical attention."

"Maybe Randolph could smoke his addiction out."

This was so ridiculous, she took me seriously. "I never thought of that. That might work. Let me write that down."

Before she could rocket out of the kitchen, Camden said, "Lottie, I hate to ask, but is Voltage Press very expensive? It's great they accepted your book, but I hope it's not going to cost you too much."

"Oh, don't worry, dear, I've done my research. I know all about self-publishing. I can't wait for a traditional publisher to accept my work. I have to carpe per deum now."

I let that one pass. "Well, congratulations."

"Thank you," she said. "And thank you for the excellent plot point. You two are just as good at solving problems as Randolph and Preston."

She dashed out.

"High praise, indeed," I said. "I'm not sure we can live up to that."

"I'm not going to even try," Camden said. "Pass the macaroni." I handed him the container. "What are those gifts on the table?"

"One is a birthday gift to Ellin from Kary, and the other is a no special reason gift to Kary from me. She and Lottie are putting on disguises and going to look for Wallace's mother this afternoon."

"I take it you don't approve?"

"You read my mind," I said. "Oh, no, sorry. Guess you didn't."

Camden hadn't lost his ability to give excellent go-to-hell looks, either.

***

After lunch, I went by the Quik-Fry. Doreen was cleaning tables, her mouth set in a determined line as if every crumb had to be obliterated. I asked her if she knew anyone named Bradley Wallace, or if Arliss had ever mentioned that name.

"No. Me and my Daddy didn't talk much. I'll ask Mama." She tucked a wayward strand of hair back under her Quik-Fry cap. "Any luck finding me a job? They're gonna cut my hours here next week, and that won't leave me a whole lot to bring home."

"Is business at the Quik-Fry that bad?" The place was always packed.

"I don't know what's going on. Something to do with the managers."

"I'm doing the best I can."

Her thin shoulders slumped. "I know. It's my fault I ain't got enough education."

"It'll be okay. Something will come up."

She toyed with the napkin dispenser on one table. "I don't know about that. My luck's always been bad."

"You've got me working for you. How bad can that be?"

This made her grin. "You are one damn sassy man, you know that? How come you're not married?"

"I've been married twice. I take responsibility for both marriages falling apart."

"It's Kary, ain't it? She's the one you really want."

I don't know how women know these things. They must have a special Relationship Radar. "Yes. But I'm going to have to prove I'm the right one for her, and part of that is getting you a good job, so you see I have a vested interest in your future."

"Doreen!" someone called.

"I gotta go." She stood on her tiptoes so she could kiss my cheek. "Thanks, Randall. It means a lot to have somebody believing in me."

\*\*\*

It was getting close to four thirty, and assuming Kary's meeting was over, it was time for me to head to Lancaster Mills to see her and Lottie in action. The tricky part would be hiding the giant white Fury. I found a place to park the car behind the dumpster at a nearby gas station and walked to the neighborhood. I chose an observation spot where I had a clear view but wouldn't be seen.

Lancaster Mills was a once-thriving textile industry that folded when the owners took their business overseas. The surrounding neighborhood was made up of apartments and small houses for the folks who worked at the mill. Most of the apartment buildings were closed and dark, tall weeds growing up to shattered windows. Faded "Condemned" signs flapped on the doors. "No Trespassing" signs hung on the chain link fence around the parking lot. However, the little houses were not in bad shape. They could have used a coat of paint and maybe some flower gardens, but everything looked dismal in the November twilight.

I expected Turbo to come chugging up the road. I expected to see Kary in an interview suit and a brown wig and Lottie in something similar. I wasn't prepared for the two hefty women who got out of a silver van. They wore drab dresses and coats and scarves on their heads. Each carried a large pocketbook. After my double take, I recognized Kary's legs, even though she was wearing thick hose and ugly brown shoes.

The women walked slowly and carefully up to one of the houses and knocked. After a long while, the door opened. They held a brief conversation with the home owner. This woman pointed to another house. There was more conversation, and then what appeared to be an exchange of thank yous and good-byes. Kary and Lottie—I could tell it was Lottie by the way she jiggled with excitement—walked to the house the woman had indicated and knocked. A man came to the door. I waited, tense, ready to leap out if he made any threatening move, but he folded his arms and nodded as he answered their questions. Then he spoke at length, finished with a curt good-by, and closed the door.

Kary and Lottie walked back to the van, got in, and drove away. I ran to my car and followed the van, not sure what they planned to do next. But the van headed back toward Food Row and Grace Street. By the time I got home, the van was gone, and Kary had shed her cocoon for jeans and a tee shirt.

"How did it go?" I asked.

Kary folded the dark clothing and coats on the piano bench, including two bulging beige leotards. "Check this out, David." She held up one of the leotards. "The theater had a couple of fat suits. With these dresses and headscarves, Lottie and I looked like Russian grandmothers. There's no way anyone could've recognized us."

Amen to that. "Where is Lottie?"

"She's returning the van she borrowed from one of her friends. We thought Turbo would be too conspicuous."

"You thought of everything. Any luck?"

"We're onto something. We didn't find Wallace's mother, but we did find a man who'd known her."

"Known her? So she's not here anymore?"

"He said she died several years ago. Her name was Bernice Allen. I asked if he knew anything about her son Bradley. That's when he really let loose. He said Bernice had no idea how to be a mother. A lot of times he could hear her screaming 'Bradley Ambrose Wallace.' Drove him nuts, he said."

"Ambrose? No wonder he turned to a life of crime."

"He said she would go off and leave Bradley home alone, she never really paid much attention to him—well, except to scream at him, and when things got really tough, she just left and never came back."

"How old was Bradley when she left him?"

"The man said around six."

So Lottie's research had been right on the money. And this information squared with what Thad Able had told me. "Did this man have any idea where Bradley was now?"

"He said he hadn't seen him in years, but that Bradley had always been reclusive. Last he heard, Bradley was living near Asheville."

"That's another thing his high school friend told me."

"And here's another telling point. The man said several times Bradley was caught tormenting the neighborhood cats. If I'm not mistaken, that's a sign a person is seriously disturbed."

"Taking his anger out on animals and then on people."

"Lottie was smart enough to ask this man what Bernice looked like. Three guesses."

"Blond."

"Yep. So now we need to find his hiding place. Any suggestions?"

"First we let Jordan know what you found out."

"Oh, the neighbor said the police had already been by asking the same questions. You know Jordan has more resources than we do."

With my thumb, I indicated the island where Camden sat reading. "We have another resource if he'd get his head out of the sand and join us."

No answer.

"I know you can hear me," I said. "On two levels."

I told Jordan what my Russian grandmothers had discovered, not mentioning them by name. He doesn't like to involve Camden, so he'd hit the ceiling if he found out Kary and Lottie had gone to Lancaster Mills in disguise, asking questions about Wallace.

He thanked me for the information.

After I ended the call, Kary found the gifts on the table. "You remembered the book, thanks, but what's this other present?"

"I saw something in Books and More and thought you'd appreciate it."

She unwrapped the box and took out the white mug with its pattern of a black magnifying glass viewing a bright red question mark, read the quote, and laughed. "'You know my methods, Watson.' You're right. It's perfect."

"You deserve a prize for your detective skills and for thinking of such a good disguise."

"I should've kept it on for you to get the full effect."

I put my arms around her. "I don't need to kiss a Russian grandma." I got in several kisses before Lottie returned.

"Kary, that was the most amazing adventure! Have you told David what we found out?"

"Yes, and now we need to find Wallace's lair."

"Oh, I have some ideas about that. Come look at my notes."

In her excitement, she almost pulled Kary up the stairs. I took a couple of deep breaths and went to the island. Camden gave me a wary glance and pretended to read his magazine.

"Perhaps you've noticed I've decided to continue investigating," I said.

"An admirable decision."

"You know as much as I like Kary helping me, I do not like the fact that a serial killer is roaming Parkland looking for blonds."

"I don't, either."

"Places Bradley Wallace might be hiding."

I said it as a challenge. Camden closed the magazine and laid it on the coffee table. "I don't know."

"I don't believe you."

He gave me the full force of his blue eyes. "You always say I'm a terrible liar. Am I lying now?"

He wasn't. I didn't want to talk to him anymore, and apparently the feeling was mutual because he took his magazine and went upstairs. I was still standing in the middle of the island when Ellin came in. Seeing her reminded me I needed to mention coming to her reunion.

She set her briefcase on the hall tree and came through the living room on her way to the kitchen. She gave me a look. "Are you lost, Randall?"

"I'm thinking of attending your reunion."

This caught her attention. "Because—?"

"I'm working on a case that may involve a member of your class."

"Arliss Padgett. Didn't you find him?"

"This is another case."

She faced me squarely. "Does this involve Cam in any way?"

"I'd like for it to, but he's gone all normal on me."

"Normal?"

"He says he isn't psychic anymore."

Camden obviously hadn't discussed this with her because he didn't want to mention falling off the roof. "What brought this on? You and I both know that's not possible."

"Wishful thinking,"

She gave me a wide-eyed stare. "He's not trying pills again, is he? I thought we were over that!"

"No pills, I promise, but he's not helpful, so he's not involved. I want to talk to Bradley Wallace and Margaret Layton. Would you be willing to point them out to me if they're at the reunion?"

Her stare narrowed. "Oh, not involved, you say? Then explain this. Lottie stopped by the PSN earlier today to take some notes on something she calls *Death From Beyond*, and proceeded to tell me all about this serial killer and how you and Cam were working on the case together and she was going to help solve the mystery."

Working on a case together. Lottie had successfully torpedoed my secret.

"So how is this not involved, Randall?"

I tried to dig out of this particular hole. "Yes, there is a serial killer, and I'm helping Jordan, but Camden is not, because he's no longer psychic, and Lottie is sort of on the case as a consultant, I guess you'd say. She had some good ideas, which she shared with me, but that's it."

Ellin's look said she could imagine what sort of good ideas Lottie would share.

"I don't know what this is about Cam and his psychic powers, or you and Lottie and my reunion and serial killers, but if anything happens that shouldn't happen, I'm holding you responsible."

"I think that covers everything."

"I mean it, Randall."

"Okay. So you'll point out Margaret and Bradley?"

"Yes. How do you plan to get in? The reunion is just for people in my high school class and their husbands or wives. I had to RSVP."

I hadn't thought about that. I assumed anyone could wander in and claim to be a former Parkland High student. Then I thought again and began to laugh. I knew exactly how to get in.

Ellin looked at me askance. "Did I say something funny?"

"Don't mind me," I said. "I've just had an apostrophe."

# Chapter Seventeen

*"Daddy Come Around"*

Lottie had done more research and discovered that Voltage would print as many copies of her books as she could afford. Friday morning, the dining room table was covered with paper of all colors, some with roughly drawn pictures.

"Voltage even offers a color cover with my choice of design," she said. "These are just my plans, you understand, so I can decide which color would look best for each book and what sort of eye-catching picture would really pull in the readers. I'm trying to think of a good image for *Web of Deceit*."

I'd go with the obvious. "How about a giant black spider and web on yellow?"

"Do you think so? What about for *The Raging Rapids*?"

Randolph and Preston going over Niagara Falls in a barrel. "Blue and white with blood in some sparkly waves."

"Oh, my gosh! That would be fantastic. What should I have for *The Opal's Curse*?"

I really needed some coffee. "A big opal shooting out purple death rays."

"Great ideas! David, have you done this sort of thing before?"

"It's my new career." I made my way into the kitchen so I wouldn't have to design covers for her entire *oeuvre*. "*Oeuvre*" first thing in the morning. Had to be worth a hundred points.

As I got my coffee I could hear her muttering to herself. When

Kary came downstairs to the dining room Lottie greeted her with a trill of delight.

"Kary, I want you to look at all these wonderful ideas David had for my book covers. What do you think about this glistening opal with the eyeball for *The Opal's Curse*? I'm going to have deadly rays shooting out from it. That was David's idea."

"Oh, definitely," Kary said. "Make sure the eye is all bloodshot with big black lashes. That'll make people stop in the bookstore."

"Bookstore?" Lottie said. "I hadn't even thought about that. I'd better find out."

Kary patiently looked at each one and made all the right comments. When she came into the kitchen, she gave me a wry smile. "I don't know why you want to continue detecting when you have such a bright future as a graphic designer."

"It's a gift I didn't know I had." She took her lunch bag out of the fridge and put it in her tote bag. "No time for breakfast this morning. I have a parent coming for a conference before school. Lottie and I made a list of possible hiding places Wallace might choose. I'll text it to you. Check with me later."

"You got it, boss."

She hurried out, calling good-by to Lottie, who was on her way upstairs to research bookstores. I sat down at the counter, wishing I had such a successful, thriving detective agency she wouldn't have to work or make ham and cheese sandwiches for her lunch.

The kitchen was quiet for about five minutes, and then Ellin came in to get her coffee.

"What's all the trash on the table?" she asked.

"Lottie's book covers."

Ellin took a sip of coffee. "I'll be glad when she moves out."

"I plan to marry Kary and find us a cozy love nest somewhere. Then you and Camden can have the whole place to yourselves."

"Cam and I will be in a nice new house that doesn't constantly need repairs or screwy tenants."

"Good luck convincing him to move."

"Oh, I will. As for what we discussed earlier, remember I am holding you responsible."

I gave her a salute. "Yes, ma'am. I am the most responsible

person in this house."

This made her laugh. "I can think of another word for you."

She made sure her travel cup was filled and left. Camden was the last to arrive in the kitchen.

"Still not psychic?" I asked.

He gave me a look and didn't answer.

I took another drink of my coffee. "Then if you're looking for something more mundane to do, Kary and Lottie have a list of serial killer hiding places we can check."

He reached in the cabinet for a box of Pop-Tarts. "Okay."

"Okay? You're actually going to help?"

"If it will shut you up, yes."

I grinned. "Does this mean Vision Man has returned to the League of Superheroes?"

He put two Pop-Tarts in the toaster. "Before you get your tights in a wad, checking possible hideouts does not require psychic ability."

"If you were still psychic and had gone along with me to Lancaster Mills, you would've picked up some great vibes. I'll bet the place is loaded with ghosts."

"Why would I want to see ghosts?"

"Because they talk to you." And to me, which made me think of Lindsey. Was she busy finding more clients for me, or was the fact Camden was being so stubborn keeping her from coming in clearly? She needed to explain what she meant by the other girl.

"Have you heard from Lindsey lately? There was someone else she wanted me to help." I wasn't surprised when he said no, so I changed the subject. "You know your sweetie is plotting a way to move you out of here."

"She will not succeed." His Pop-Tarts popped up, and he put them on a plate. "Is that the illustrated adventures of Randolph and Preston on the table?"

"Lottie's in the midst of designing her book covers."

"Can we possibly leave before we're called upon to pose?"

\*\*\*

We were not called upon to pose. After breakfast, Camden joined me in my office. We were going over the list Kary and Lottie had compiled when Jordan called, wanting me to bring Camden to the station. Camden was reluctant to go, but Jordan didn't have another hunk of hair or a torn article of clothing for him to hold.

"Take a look at these pictures, Cam." Jordan spread several grainy photos out on his desk. "I want to know if this is Wallace."

Since identifying someone from a picture could be considered a non-psychic activity, Camden agreed.

"Where did you get these?" I asked.

"We've been checking surveillance cameras from all over the city. This footage is from a convenience store near the site of the last murder. This guy fits the description, but no one at the store could identify him. And that's not all." Jordan ran his hand through his hair, making the stiff bristles stand even straighter. "According to the Asheville PD, a few years ago, they had two still unsolved murders, both blond women."

"Anything from Summer Lakes?"

"Neighbors there said Wallace and his wife had a screaming fight one morning and she left right then. Probably saved her life. They said Wallace moved out the next day and they never saw either of them again."

"So he moves to Asheville and takes out his anger on other blond women."

"That's what it looks like. He keeps evading us, and now he's gone to ground." He turned his attention to Camden. "Getting anything, Cam?"

"I can't tell for sure if it's Wallace or not."

Jordan looked surprised. "This sort of thing is usually easy for you."

"Not anymore." Jordan started to say something, but Camden continued. "You're always saying psychic evidence doesn't hold up in court, so I can't see that it matters if I have some special power to identify this man."

Jordan doesn't get mad at Camden, but I could tell he was having trouble keeping his temper. "Well, it sure as hell matters to the women he's terrorized and killed and to the families left behind."

Camden had the grace to look ashamed. "I'm sorry. I just can't help you anymore."

Jordan took a deep breath. "Okay, look. You're still recovering from that bad fall and maybe your brain just needs to recalibrate. You didn't get any vibes from the photos, that's okay. We'll catch this guy." He turned to me. "You got anything else for me, Randall?"

I decided not to mention my reunion plan, hoping I wouldn't have to call in the big guns unless absolutely necessary.

"You get any more information, anything at all, you call me. You, too, Cam."

When we got in the Fury, I said, "That was Wallace, wasn't it?"

"Yes."

"Anything else?"

"No. Honestly, no."

He looked so dejected, I didn't press for more details. We went to Janice's and ordered some hot dogs and fries. I got a cola for me and a large vanilla milkshake for Camden. When he'd had a good drink, I called Jordan and told him that the man in the photos was indeed Bradley Wallace.

"Cam change his mind?"

"Not exactly," I said. "It came to him in the car."

"Delayed reaction?"

"Guilty conscience. We'll sort it out." Jordan thanked me and I ended the call. Janice stopped by our table with our order.

"Feeling okay?" she asked Camden.

"Yes, thanks," he said, but he was far from okay. Janice thought so, too, but she just nodded and indicated the milkshake.

"Let me know when you need a refill," she said and moved on to the next table.

Camden found something intriguing in the depths of his milkshake. I tapped on the table to get his attention.

"Look. You're doing your best not to be psychic, but you might as well accept it and move on. Taking pills doesn't work, falling off the roof doesn't work. You're stuck with it, just like I'm stuck with finding things and people and serial killers."

I wasn't sure how he'd react to my attempt at psychoanalysis, but as I figured, he was as tired of all the drama as I was. He pushed the milkshake away and sighed a weary sigh. "I just want—well, maybe I don't know what I want."

"You don't have to decide everything now. Help me catch this guy."

"Do you have any idea how to do that?"

"As a matter of fact, I have a plan to catch Mr. Clairol that works with or without your psychic help. Convenient, huh?"

"I'd like to hear this plan," he said.

"At the reunion, when you and Ellin get name tags, I need you to slip me one."

"I can do that."

"Since we now have to communicate the old fashioned way, I'll let you in on it. Then you can tell me it's brilliant." I explained my plan.

He had to grin. "It's brilliant," he said.

***

Camden called Jordan to apologize and to confirm that the man in the photos was Wallace. He agreed to come back to the station and look at more footage. We got into the Fury, but before I started the car, a call came in from Kary.

"I asked about a cafeteria job for Doreen, but unfortunately, there aren't any available. Without a high school diploma or GED, I doubt she would qualify, anyway. We might look into getting her in a training program of some kind." I heard children's voices in the background. Kary answered. "Settle down, class. I'll be right there. Are you checking out the places on my list, David?"

"Camden and I are helping the police with their inquiries."

"Does that mean Cam is psychic again?"

"For now. Talk to you later." I started the car and the CD player picked up at the next song which played for a few minutes before sputtering to a halt. A voice said, "David Randall."

Camden gave me a startled glance. I raised my eyebrows. "I know you heard that."

"David Randall."

"Speaking," I said.

"Yes," said the voice. "I want justice for myself and for the others."

"Who are you? What can I do?"

"Look in the book. You'll see. You'll understand."

What is it about ghosts and riddles? "What book?"

"The yearbook," Camden said. "Isn't that right, Yvonne?"

The voice sighed in relief. "Yes. Thank you. Show him."

The song popped back on so suddenly we both jumped. I switched it off and waited for Camden to process what had happened. No wonder the voice came in clearly this time. He had to be here, and he had to admit that fall hadn't knocked the psychic out of him. I needed a few minutes, too. I was still getting used to the idea of being on call to the departed.

"So," I said as casually as possible. This had to be the other girl, the one Lindsey wanted me to help. "Yvonne, is it? What do you think?"

He took a deep breath and blew it out. "I think we ought to help her."

***

Camden looked at more pictures, pointing out which ones were Wallace. There weren't many, and in every one, Wallace had a borrowed or stolen hoodie or baseball cap pulled down low to hide his features. Jordan took notes on where the photos were taken and texted them to his officers.

"We don't have a lot to go on, so every bit helps," he said. "Wallace is extremely careful. The only evidence we've found so far—hair, blood, even DNA—belongs to his victims, but it's only a matter of time before he makes a mistake." He typed more notes into his computer. "Okay, Cam, that's all for now, thanks very much. Anything else, Randall?"

I took out my phone. "I can send you a list of possible hide-outs."

"Sure, I'll have a look. But trust me, we are looking every-where."

Once this was done, Camden and I went home. When we got to the house, we took Ellin's yearbook and looked for Yvonne. We found a picture of a beautiful blond girl on the In Memoriam page. Further investigation on the internet revealed that Yvonne Thompson had been murdered and her killer never caught.

I closed the yearbook. "Looks like Wallace started earlier than we thought."

Now I had three clients to answer to, Kary, Lindsey, and Yvonne.

# Chapter Eighteen

*"Papa, Won't You Dance With Me?"*

Ellin's fifteen-year senior reunion was held Saturday night in the Parkland High School gym and decorated, Ellin assured us, exactly the same as Prom Night, which meant a glitter ball and crepe paper streamers and a band cranking out the tunes from back in her high school days. With the music pulsing around us, we made our way through the fake smiles and extra pounds. I'd skipped my high school's ten-year reunion and didn't plan on attending any others. We'd been bussed in from dozens of little Minnesota towns to one big high school in Marshall. I'd made decent grades and played a bit of football, but most of my high school years were a blur. My classmates were now farmers, schoolteachers, and shopkeepers, not like this glittery overweight bunch of Parkland socialites.

I saw the pride in Ellin's eyes as she introduced Camden to her old classmates. Since he was the best looking man there, aside from myself, she had a right to brag a little. Most of the people knew Camden or had heard of him.

He'd palmed the nametag I needed off the registration table and passed it to me. I'd attached it to my lapel.

"You see Margaret or Bradley yet?" I asked Ellin.

"Not yet, but I just saw Doris Henway, and she's on husband number four."

"That's good, Ellin. I'm very happy for you. Would you please look around?"

"Give me a minute."

She finally pointed out a stylish woman with blond hair, but this blond hair was cut very short and spiky. "There's Margaret. I'm almost certain."

I approached the woman and smiled. "Margaret Layton?"

She turned and smiled back. I saw her nametag, "Margaret Layton Douglas," and the small photo of how she appeared in high school. Gone was the vacant-eyed teen with shoulder length fluffy hair. This modern Margaret Layton was cool and confident. She peered at my nametag, did a double take, and her smile broadened.

"The years have certainly been kind to you, Arliss."

"Thank you, but I'm here under false pretenses. My name's really David Randall. I'm a private investigator, and I need your help."

Various emotions flickered across her face. "My help? Whatever for?"

"I'm not sure if you're aware of a serial killer the *Parkland Herald* is calling Mr. Clairol. I think he may have been a classmate of yours."

She wasn't alarmed by this news. "Really? What makes you say that?"

"He's obsessed with a woman named Margaret."

"You think I'm that Margaret? There must be thousands of Margarets in Parkland."

Jordan had told me. "Two hundred and six. Was there anyone in high school who hung around but never got up enough nerve to approach you?"

Now her smile was wry. "There were lots of them, Mr. Randall. I was pretty bubble-headed back then, boy-crazy, dated a lot. I had plenty of admirers."

"No one particularly weird?"

"Everyone was weird in high school."

"Name three."

She took a sip of her drink and sighed as if she were back in algebra class and had been asked to solve a word problem. "Oh, I don't know. Vince Dobbins, Bradley Wallace, Minnie Goins." She grinned at my nametag. "Arliss Padgett."

"Any of them here tonight?"

"I think I saw Bradley's name on the list. I'm not sure what happened to him after graduation. Vince became a pharmacist, and Minnie became a lap dancer." The amused tone cooled. "You don't think there's any danger involved, do you?"

I looked at her boyish haircut and thought of Mr. Clairol's long fingers playing with his victim's hair. "It wouldn't hurt to be cautious."

"I wish I could help, but suppose this guy's just fixated on the name Margaret? Maybe he's really crazy about a Cathy and just likes to call her Margaret. If he's a nut, he'll do anything, right? He may not even be a member of this class."

I thought of Camden's reaction to the yearbook page. "I'm pretty sure he is. Point out Bradley Wallace, if you can."

She gazed around the crowed room and shook her head. The silvery reflections of the revolving glitter ball bounced off jewelry and made hazy patterns on faces. "I don't see him. I'll ask around."

I gave her one of my cards, one with only my name and cell phone number. "Let's play it safe. If he gets in touch with you, call me and call the police."

"All right." She slipped my card into her little jeweled purse. "I live in Abbington now, but I'm staying with some friends in Parkland for the week. Let me give you their number. I'd like to know if I need to take extra precautions."

I put her friends' number into my phone and went back to Camden and Ellin. They were talking with a plump cheerful woman who looked familiar to me, although I couldn't place her until I heard what she was saying. Then I knew a perfectly good lie was about to go up in smoke and Camden along with it.

"You probably don't remember me," she said to Camden, "but I was on duty the day you were brought in. I'm so glad you're all right. You're very lucky. Not everybody falls off the roof and lives to tell the tale."

Damn, I thought, seeing Ellin's gaze slew around.

"Falls off the roof?" she said, her voice deceptively calm.

"Yes, it was quite an accident," the woman said. "If that big pile of leaves hadn't been there—"

"I didn't want Ellie to worry," Camden said in a vain attempt to save his life.

Way too late for that. "Oh, I want to hear all the details," Ellin said. "Every single one."

So the woman told her. All the while, Ellin slowly turned to stone, Camden slowly turned to jelly, and I slowly turned toward the door, hoping to escape unnoticed. After the damage was done, the woman spied another old chum and went off to spread more sunshine.

"Randall," Ellin said in a voice like a knife through rawhide.

I should have known I couldn't get away unscathed, but I gave it a try. "I was at the Quik-Fry. You can't blame this one on me."

She swung around to Camden. "You fell off the *roof?*"

Several people turned to stare in our direction. Ellin brought her voice down a few thousand degrees.

"You fell off the roof and you didn't *tell* me?"

"Ellie—" he began.

"What the hell were you thinking?" She had to freeze a smile as a classmate strolled past. Then she snagged Camden's arm and propelled him toward the door. "You and I are going to have a serious talk right now."

He cast a look over his shoulder that reminded me of the time he almost drowned. Can't save you this time, pal.

I would probably never see Camden again, so I had to find Bradley Wallace on my own. I worked the room until I found someone who pointed him out. He did not fit the profile or match any part of the police composite sketch. He was bald, but much too short to have been on the Dynamite Bears basketball team, short and smiling as if he lived for high school reunions.

"Bradley Wallace?"

He turned his smile my way, glanced at my nametag, and then shook my hand vigorously. "Arliss Padgett, you old son of a gun! How've you been?"

"Just fine," I said. "Who are you, really?"

The beaming face fell. "Aww, how'd you guess? He said nobody'd remember him."

"Because I'm not Arliss Padgett, as anyone who went to Parkland High could tell you. What's the deal?"

"Oh, it's not a deal. It's what I do. This guy Wallace paid me three hundred and fifty dollars to impersonate him at the reunion. He said nobody would remember him, and nobody would look the same, anyway." He frowned. "I've been able to fool everybody else."

"Sorry to spoil your fun. You mind telling me why Wallace didn't want to come himself?"

"Same reason Arliss Padgett didn't want to come, I'll bet. How much did he pay you?"

"Nothing." I dug out my ID to show him I was a licensed private investigator. "I'm working tonight."

"Whoa, hey!" He backed off, alarmed. "I haven't done anything wrong! There's nothing illegal about this!"

"Calm down. I'm trying to locate the real Bradley Wallace. There's a lot of money involved. An inheritance. I was hoping he'd be here tonight. Can you tell me how to get in touch with him? Are you supposed to meet him later and tell him about the reunion?"

"He said he'd get in touch with me. I never actually met him. We did all our business over the phone."

"You got a number?"

"He called me."

"His number didn't show up?"

"The caller ID said 'Unknown.'"

"You see why I've had such a time reaching him? He's a very cautious man." I couldn't believe I might actually have a way to find Wallace. I dug another one of my Inheritance Specialist name and number cards out of my pocket and handed it to my new contact. "Do me a favor. The next time he calls, give him my number. Tell him I'll respect his privacy, but he needs to know about the money. There may be something in it for you, too."

"Me?"

"If Mr. Wallace is this cautious, he may hire you to deal with me."

"Oh, yeah." For some reason, this calmed him down. "Well, I'd be glad to be the middle man."

"So what do people call you when you're not impersonating Bradley Wallace?"

"Stuart King."

"How did Wallace know to get in touch with you, Mr. King? Do you advertise in *Impersonators Weekly*?"

He grinned, unoffended, and reached into his jacket pocket. "I guess he saw one of my cards." He handed one to me.

"'King Enterprises,'" I read. "'No job too small. Characters for your parties, buffets, supermarket openings. Reasonable rates.'"

"I have one on every bulletin board in town," Stuart King said. "I get a lot of birthday parties mostly."

Now things started to make sense. "So you're a Rent-A-Clown?"

"A clown, Santa, the Easter Bunny, your long lost Uncle Jack. You name it. Believe it or not, I've been to lots of reunions. Usually some woman doesn't want to go alone, so I pretend to be her husband or significant other."

"You make a living this way?"

"It's more of a side line. I have a regular job at Super Food."

I tucked his card into my pocket."How did Wallace pay you, if you don't mind me asking?"

"He mailed it to me. Four hundred dollar bills."

"No return address, I'll bet."

"No. I guess it is odd, once you think of it."

Odd, but not surprising. Wallace did not want to leave a trail of any kind. "This is all very interesting, Mr. King. Be sure to let Mr. Wallace know I'm trying to reach him."

"Sure will."

I thought I'd better go sweep up what was left of Camden. I found him and Ellin in earnest conversation outside, standing away from the knots of smokers. He'd said something right, because she had her arms around his waist, not his neck, and was giving him one of those soulful looks that always take me by surprise. I've been married twice, and I've had countless girlfriends, but nobody ever looked at me that way, although I have to say Kary's working up to it.

"I'm glad you're all right," she said. "But honestly, Cam, you've got to be more careful! This is why we need a new house. These repairs are going to be the death of you."

Made sense to me. I knew the only way Camden would leave the house would be feet first.

"The house is in good shape," he said. "I promise I'll be more careful."

From the look in Ellin's eyes, I knew she was only giving in for now. "Okay." She kissed him. "I have an idea. Why don't we go back to our old house and see if we can make that wallpaper curl?"

***

When I got home a few hours later, I found Camden on the island sofa.

"What's wrong?" I asked, thinking he'd had a relapse.

"Ellie's still a bit annoyed."

"Sorry. I thought you were over the worst of it after that nurse spilled the beans."

As usual, he defended his wife. "She'll be all right in the morning. She's tired and she's a year older, and that depresses her. We'll work it out."

I sat down in the blue arm chair. "Well, I had better luck this evening. Like Arliss Padgett, who was conveniently in jail, our suspect didn't attend the reunion but sent someone in his place, a fellow named Stuart King." I handed him King's card. "See if you can get anything off that."

Camden held the card for a moment. "Does he work in a circus?"

"Mr. King works at Super Food, but his side hustle is being a clown for parties and impersonating people who'd rather be somewhere else. There's a good chance I can use him to get to the killer. Anything else?"

Camden returned the card. "Just clowns and balloons."

"Maybe you're not quite up to speed yet. You'll need to shake his hand. Or hold one of his giant clown shoes. I'll bet he has some." We'd left the yearbook on the coffee table. I found the picture of Bradley Wallace. Somewhere along the line he'd ditched

"Ambrose." "Stuart didn't fit my idea of an evil henchman, but you never know."

"You warned Margaret."

"Yes, and I think she understood the danger."

He glanced up. "Speaking of danger, I'd better go see if I can forge a new peace agreement."

"Careful. She'll have all your stuff in a U-Haul before sunrise."

"And leave Elizabeth Singer and Tubbs with you? I don't think so."

He met Kary on the stairs as she was coming down. She wished him luck and joined me in the island.

"I want to hear all about the reunion. Did Bradley Wallace show up? Did Margaret?"

I invited Kary into the kitchen for a snack and an update. I took the jar of peanut butter out of the cabinet. "You know I went to the reunion as Arliss. Wallace also sent a ringer, a fellow by the name of Stuart King. Stuart said Wallace called him. He doesn't have a number, and he's never met Wallace."

"Was Margaret there? I hoped you warned her."

"Yes, I warned her. Her hair is very short and stylish. Not much for Wallace to get his hands on, but I would not want to take any chances." I brought the peanut butter and a box of crackers to the counter. "She's staying with friends, so she's not alone."

"How did Stuart King get mixed up with Wallace?"

I showed her Stuart's card. "Stuart's one of those guys you call when you need a clown for your kid's birthday party or a date to your cousin's wedding."

"Did you tell him about Wallace's phony inheritance?"

"Yes, and he bought the whole story." I gestured toward the upper floor with my peanut butter knife. "Were you home for the fireworks display?"

"I couldn't help but overhear. How did Ellin find out?"

"The nurse who was on duty just happened to be a member of Ellin's class."

"Ooo, bad luck." Kary peeled the plastic from the sleeve of crackers. "We knew she'd find out eventually, though."

"It gives her more ammunition regarding the house."

"Cam will never want to live anywhere else."

I made a peanut butter cracker and handed it to her. "What about you? Do you want to stay here, or would you like a place of your own?" Though how I could afford a house was a problem for another day.

"I go back and forth on that. Sometimes I think it would be nice to have my own place, but I'm pretty content with the way things are right now. What about you?"

What about me? I hadn't caught Wallace. I hadn't found a job for Doreen. I hadn't completely decided to continue my agency. But I was sitting in the kitchen with the beautiful, intelligent, forthright woman I wasn't about to lose.

"If you're here, I'm here," I said.

# Chapter Nineteen

*"Papa's Got a Brand New Bag"*

Sunday morning, I looked up from my computer to see a brown van turn into our driveway and park behind the Fury. To my amazement and concern, Stuart King got out and walked up the porch steps. How did he get my address? My card only listed my phone number. I met him at the door, and he looked just as amazed to see me.

"Hey," he said. "Uh, do you live here?"

"Mr. King, how did you get this address?"

"From some folks at the reunion," he said. "They were real helpful. When I mentioned I was looking for an apartment, they said the Camdens ran a boarding house at 302 Grace Street and might have a room."

Alarm bells went off all through my insides. Was he telling the truth, or had he contacted Wallace to let him know a snoopy detective was on his trail? I stepped out onto the porch and closed the door behind me. "Sorry, no vacancies at the moment. I can put your name on the list."

"Well, I wanted to talk to you, anyway," he said. "Wallace called me late last night. I gave him your message, and he wants to know the details."

Finally, a break in this case, but I needed to get Stuart King out of here right away. "The details are confidential, but I'll be glad to meet him anywhere he likes." Except here. No way in hell I'd want that maniac anywhere near Grace Street. Even though the connection to Wallace was slight, Stuart had to leave. "How about we go down to Perkie's and discuss this? You know where that is? Coffee shop on the corner of the park?"

"Sure," he said. "I'll meet you there."

Camden's peace plans with Ellin had fallen through, and he'd spent the night on the sofa and was only now awake. When I came to the island, he sat up and pushed his hair out of his eyes.

"Emergency situation," I told him. "Stuart King showed up at our door, and it better have been a coincidence."

Camden was instantly alert. "If he's had any contact with Wallace—" The thought of what might happen made his voice quit.

"Exactly. I redirected him to Perkie's. You picked an excellent time to become psychic. Come shake his hand."

At Perkie's, I found a table in the corner, and after ordering a coffee for myself and a Coke for Camden, we greeted Stuart King and sat down. The man looked completely harmless. With Arliss in jail, Wallace had very little time to find another go-between for the reunion. I hoped Stuart had been a spur of the moment choice and not someone directly involved with the murders.

Well, I would soon know. "Mr. King, this is Camden. Camden, Stuart King."

Camden smiled as he shook Stuart's hand. "Nice to meet you."

"I told him there were no vacancies right now."

"Yes, sorry about that, Stuart." He regarded the man calmly.

I took a deep breath. If Stuart had been dangerous, if he'd had anything to do with the murders, Camden would have been vibrating like a tuning fork.

"Can you tell me anything else about Wallace?" I asked.

Stuart put two sugars into his coffee. "Like I said, I haven't actually seen him, and the caller ID still says 'Unknown.' It's hard to tell much about a person over the phone. His voice is kinda monotone, but doesn't have a particular accent. He sounds like a regular guy."

Yeah, a regular guy who plays with dead hair. "It's important that I get in touch with him before the twenty-third. He's going to have to sign some papers before I can hand over any of the money." I lowered my voice. "I'm telling you this in strictest confidence, you understand. This money is well in excess of three hundred thousand dollars."

Stuart whistled appreciatively. "Not a bad little chunk of dough."

"You might mention that to Wallace the next time he calls."

"Sure will."

"If Wallace prefers, he can call my number, the one I gave you. I'd be glad to give him more details." With Jordan Finley and the entire Parkland P.D. listening in.

"I'll pass along the info."

"What exactly did he want to know about the reunion?"

"Oh, nothing much. He wanted to know if certain people were there and what they looked like now."

"Did he happen to mention Margaret Layton?"

"Oh, yeah, he was particularly interested in hearing about her."

"She's changed quite a bit, I think."

"Still an attractive woman. I can see why she was popular in high school."

"Did he say anything else about her?"

Stuart thought it over. "No. He wanted to know if she was there and still as beautiful. Wanted to know about her hair, actually."

I gave Camden a casual glance and feigned innocence. "Her hair?"

"Yeah, asked me all sorts of questions about her hair. Seemed a little annoyed she'd cut it short. I told him it looked great, very sophisticated. He hung up soon after that." He took a big drink of coffee. "You'll excuse me if I have to go. Got to be at the Super Food in about thirty minutes. Let me know if you have any openings at your house, Camden."

"I will," he said.

"Well?" I asked as soon as Stuart was gone. "It didn't seem like you saw anything threatening."

"I didn't," he said. "He really doesn't know what's going on."

"Let's keep it that way."

\*\*\*

When we got back to the house, Lottie had spread more cover art on the dining room table.

" David, if you have just a minute, what do you think of this for *Indignant Exposure*?" She held up a picture of a knife dripping blood surrounded by huge question marks.

My cover choice for a book titled *Indignant Exposure* would have been a group of gray-haired church ladies clutching their pearls and staring, affronted, at a scantily-clad bathing beauty. "That's perfect."

"I knew I was on the right track with the question marks." She gathered her papers into an untidy stack. "Kary said you met a man last night at the reunion who'd actually been in contact with Wallace. Do you want us to shadow him?"

"No, thank you. I don't want him anywhere near any of you."

"Oh, but we'd be in those wonderful disguises. How would he even know us?"

"Sorry, Lottie I'm not taking any chances."

She looked disappointed. "I suppose that's wise."

"Is Kary up?" She and Camden always went to church.

"Yes, and Ellin is, too."

Right on cue, Ellin came down the stairs, headed for work. Yes, even on Sunday. She looked sharp in her gray suit and blue crescent moon jewelry. She didn't say anything, but gave Camden and me a quick disapproving glance as she went out. I was very glad she hadn't seen Stuart King. He would take more explaining than I was prepared for this morning.

Kary was next down the stairs, dressed for church and readjusting one of her earrings.

"We may have a problem," I told her. "Stuart King was here this morning, looking for a room. Seems some of Ellin's school friends remembered Camden ran a boarding house."

"That is not good news," she said.

"Nope, but I steered him to Perkie's, and fortunately, Camden was available to shake his hand. He appears to be an innocent go-between. Wallace will either call him or me about the inheritance."

"That's a relief. What did he say about Wallace?"

"Wallace specifically wanted to know about Margaret's hair and seemed miffed when Stuart told him she'd cut it short."

"Sounds like our serial killer."

"I told Stuart that Wallace's inheritance was over three hundred thousand dollars. Think that'll lure him out? I'll have Jordan and company waiting. Are you and Lottie going on patrol today?"

"No, she's working on her book covers." She sighed. "I had hoped to get back to the clinic, but they don't need me."

"Don't need you? I would think they'd need all the help they can get."

"They recently hired another counselor. They were very nice, thanked me, and said they'd be in touch, but explained they have to have licensed people on hand. Since I plan to be licensed in oh, maybe ten years, I'll have to wait."

"You will not have to wait ten years," Camden said.

"Is this Psychic Camden talking?" she asked with an impish grin.

"Maybe. Maybe you're smart enough and determined enough to make it in five, what do you think about that?"

"I think," she said, "that you'd better change clothes or we'll be late for church. Are you coming with us, David?"

Usually I do, because it's important to Kary, but I was too concerned about Stuart King's connection to Bradley Wallace to sit quietly in a pew for an hour or more.

"I'm going to talk to Jordan," I said.

\*\*\*

Before I went to the police station, I used the public records database to do a background check on Stuart King. There wasn't even a traffic ticket. But even with Camden's verification I wanted to be sure, so Jordan agreed to also do a background check.

"Shouldn't take long," he said, clicking away at his computer. "Especially if King didn't set Cam off into Visionland. And you say he wasn't able to get in touch with Wallace? Did he try reverse call?"

"As far as I can tell, the reunion was just another job, and even if he had Wallace's number, King had no reason to call him back."

"And you went to the reunion as Arliss. I'm surprised he sent in an RSVP."

"Me, too. That's when I thought maybe that was his old school pal Wallace's idea. With Arliss in jail, our serial killer had to find someone else quickly. King has his posters and cards up all over town."

Jordan sat up and peered at his computer screen. "Well, there's nothing criminal here. Still, we can monitor his activity. If Wallace contacts him again, he may want to meet him somewhere. If there's a chance King can lead us to Wallace, I don't want to bring him in yet. Wallace could be watching."

"I have another idea," I said. "Let Arliss out. Has he been formally charged with assault?"

"No. Porter didn't press charges."

"He won't trust you, but he might talk to me. If you can release him, I'll bet he leads us right to Wallace."

Jordan was silent a moment, thinking. "Let me see what I can work out."

I thought of Doreen and her mother alone in the trailer park. "It might be a good idea to have someone patrol the Padgetts' trailer park. Wallace might go after Doreen or her mother."

Jordan agreed. He picked up his phone. "Either way, Arliss has served his time."

Thirty minutes later, I was parked in front of the police station ready to welcome Arliss Padgett back into society. For a man who'd been given his freedom, he did not look all that thrilled. He glanced at the Fury apprehensively.

"Need a ride?"

He hadn't lost his sneer. "What's it to you?"

"Okay, walk home." I started the car.

"Hold on." He opened the passenger side door. "You can drop me off at Meechum's."

As much as I hated letting his sorry ass touch the Fury's leather seat, I told him to get in and buckle up.

"I suppose you want something," he said.

"Why did you help Bradley Wallace?"

He shrugged. "Brought him food sometimes, newspapers."

"Why? You must have known what he was doing."

"Nah. Just being neighborly. We went to school together."

"So you played on the same basketball team?"

He looked at me as if I were crazy.

"I don't believe in your better nature," I said. "Or the bond of old high school ties. I think he killed Pauline Raterman to keep you in line. It was his way of saying, you do as I say, or your daughter's next. Doreen's blond, in case you've forgotten."

Arliss hunched a scrawny shoulder. "What makes you think I care anything about her? It's my own skin I'm interested in. And what makes you think I care about what happened to Pauline? It's her own fault she messed with him."

"Wait a minute," I said. "She messed with Wallace? What do you mean?"

"She was yelling at him. Told him to get off her property. Should've kept her mouth shut."

Several pieces of this puzzle fell into place. "You saw Wallace kill her. That's what he's holding over you."

Another shrug.

"You lied to the police. You were there that day."

"So what?"

"Why was Wallace in your trailer park, anyway? Why were you there?"

I knew Arliss wouldn't have come to see Hazel or Doreen. Then another piece clicked into place. "You were there to see Pauline, weren't you?"

Arliss stared out the window for a while and then suddenly let forth a stream of words. "Wallace showed up at Meechum's 'bout a week ago, wanting to know where Margaret was. I told him I didn't know. He said why not? I said, I don't keep up with every jerk and bitch I went to high school with. He told me I'd better find her. I said, didn't you get the announcement about the reunion? She's bound to be there. He said, I want her address. I said, wait and ask her, you moron. He didn't like that. Next thing I knowed, he shows up at Pauline's same time I'm there. Pauline's yelling and wanting to know who he is and what's he doing, and he stared at her and next thing she's laying in the dirt with a skint head. Then he don't even go to the reunion, right? He sends some fat guy. Least that what I heard."

"Listen to me," I said. "If Wallace approaches you or calls you and asks you to do something, say yes, play along, and call me, understand?"

"I don't want nothing more to do with that nutbar."

"All you have to do is call me."

"What's in it for me?"

"You get to live."

"Naw, I mean moneywise."

"You get to live, and you get to keep your hair."

He gave me a furtive glance as if he expected me to go for his scalp. "Yeah, well, maybe."

"Help me catch him. We'll put him behind bars, and he won't bother you anymore."

"Is there a reward?"

"Could be."

Arliss considered this.

"I'll talk to Jordan Finley," I said. "There may be some money."

His eyes narrowed. "Ain't splitting it with you."

"You can have it all if you call me and we catch Wallace."

I pulled up in front of Meechum's, a bar on the west side of town. As Arliss started to get out of the car, I handed him one of my cards. He tossed it back at me.

"I got one of those, remember?"

\*\*\*

"So he did witness Pauline Raterman's murder," Jordan said when I related the news. "If Wallace thinks he ratted on him, that's the last you'll see of Padgett."

"If you've got a tail on him it might save his worthless life."

"Yeah. Pretty soon everybody in Parkland will have their own personal police officer. Worth it if we catch this killer."

*** 

Lottie had finished designing most of her book covers and moved her cover art operation upstairs, so the dining room table was clear. We had plenty of church food left for lunch. Camden wanted macaroni and cheese and apple pie with ice cream, while Kary and I opted for ham casserole and cake. Lottie decided on a pimento cheese sandwich and sugar cookies.

I told them what Jordan and I had planned for Stuart and Arliss.

Lottie's eyes sparkled. "So you've set things in motion."

"I hope so."

"Now we'll have to see if Wallace takes the bait. This is really exciting."

Nerve-wracking was how I'd describe it. Despite Camden's assurance Stuart was harmless, I would not relax until Wallace was caught.

Kary picked up the large plastic bowl of macaroni and cheese. "Cam, do you want to put some of this food in smaller containers?"

"Yes, thanks."

"I know Ellin found out about your roof dive. I hate to say it, but this is what happens when you try to hide the truth. No wonder she steamed out of the house this morning."

"Yes, I know. And I will pay."

"I'm so sorry things didn't work out at the clinic," Lottie said to Kary.

Kary opened the cabinet that held all the plastic containers and chose one from the stack. "I can't let it get me down. There are still a lot of options left. Plus I have all those children at school to look after. When is Ellin going to have her first baby, Cam?"

"May."

"So you are in tune with the universe again?"

"As in tune as I'll ever be."

My cell phone rang. I really wasn't expecting results so fast and was caught off-guard. The caller ID said "Unknown." The voice was low, unremarkable. One might even say monotone. "I'm trying to reach David Randall."

"Speaking."

"I was informed you have some money for me."

Hairs along the back of my neck began to prickle. I was almost certain I was talking to the infamous Mr. Clairol. "Yes, that's right." I motioned to the phone and mouthed, "It's him." "You'll need to come by my office and sign a few papers," I said into the phone.

"How do I know this isn't some sort of swindle?"

"I assure you this is legitimate," I said. "However, if you have questions, you can check with Jordan Finley of the Parkland Police Department. He specializes in fraud and will be glad to verify whatever I tell you."

There was a long pause. "That won't be necessary. How much money?"

"It's a substantial amount. I don't feel comfortable discussing it over the phone." If Stuart told you what I hope he did, you know the answer, and you're going to have to come and get it, you psycho.

"Who has left me this inheritance?"

I made some appropriate shuffling noises on the table. "I have that right here. A cousin on your father's side, deceased as of November twelfth."

Silence.

"May I set up a time and place for us to meet? Completely at your convenience?"

"I'll think about it," he said and ended the call.

I immediately tried every trick I knew to reverse call. Nothing. For a few moments, I didn't move. Listening to the guy's voice had given me the creeps.

"Did it work? Kary asked. "Did you get his number?"

"No," I said. Damn! I wanted to catch this guy. I wanted to get him off the streets before he scalped another blond. I wanted to find him. I called Jordan and told him what happened.

"No luck on the reverse call," I said. "He must be using one of those throwaway phones."

"Yeah, a burn phone," Jordan said. "Anyone can buy one at

Walmart. But he said he'd think about your offer?"

"Yes."

"Get him to agree on a meeting place. We'll be there in full force."

"Do you have anyone watching out for Margaret Layton? She's staying with friends. I've got their number, and I'll call and ask for their address."

"I'll put someone on that right now."

I gave him the number Margaret Layton had given me, ended the call, and then called Margaret.

"It's David Randall from the reunion," I said. "Those extra precautions you talked about? It's time to take them."

"Are you serious?" she said. "Are you telling me Bradley Wallace is really this serial killer?"

"That's what it looks like. If you'll give me the address of your friends' house, I've asked the police to send someone to patrol that neighborhood."

"They live at 1225 Sunnyside Avenue."

"Is that where you are now?"

"I'm out shopping with my friends, and we're going to eat lunch at Max's."

"How long are you planning to be in town?" I asked.

"I'm going home Monday," she said.

I hoped Wallace wouldn't decide to follow her all the way to Abbington. "Just don't go anywhere alone." I thanked her and hung up. I sent Jordan the Sunnyside Avenue address and turned to Camden, Kary, and Lottie, who had been listening in tense silence to all my calls. "Margaret's with her friends. I'm going over to her friends' house to assure myself everything's okay."

Kary finished loading the plastic container with the last of the macaroni and snapped the lid shut. "I'd come with you, but I need to pick up Ellin's birthday cake."

"Okay, Camden, you can come with me. There might be some useful vibes in Margaret's neighborhood."

That was the plan before Ellin arrived unexpectedly and informed Camden that he was going house hunting with her.

He wrapped the remaining ham biscuits in a piece of aluminum foil. "Ellie, I have no intention of moving, so looking at houses is pointless."

"Everything's under control at the PSN," she said. "This would be a perfect afternoon to go to a couple of Open House events in Starwood."

"We've seen the houses in Starwood."

"Not all of them."

He replaced the cover on the apple pie. "How many more are there?"

"There's a Colonial style I'm interested in and a very nice Italian villa."

"I'm sure those will be just as soulless as the others," Camden said and then realized his mistake.

Ellin's expression was triumphant. "Well, now that you're psychic again, you can come and find out for sure, can't you? I'm going to call the PSN and make sure Reg hasn't taken over the network with one of his stupid program ideas. I'll give you thirty minutes to finish whatever you're doing. No arguments. You know you owe me big time."

Ellin went into the living room to make her call. Camden stacked the dirty lunch plates. "Payday has arrived."

"Why don't I come with you?" Lottie said. "I could do some research for *Mansion of Death*."

Kary picked up the empty tea glasses. "You're always saying you don't see Ellin enough. Think of it as a date."

"Now that you're back on track, tell her those houses are haunted," I said. "Or if you like, I could throw you off the roof."

"Excellent suggestions," Camden said wryly. "But I think I can handle it."

# Chapter Twenty

## *"Daddy, Don't You Walk So Fast"*

First I drove to Max's, a small Mexican restaurant in the May-field Shopping Center. I waited until Margaret and her two friends came out of the restaurant, all carrying shopping bags. I watched as they crossed the parking lot to their car. They got in and drove off without incident. I followed them to Sunnyside Avenue. When I was sure they were safely in Margaret's friends' house, I started back up the street. I didn't see a patrol car, but I did see a light brown Nissan Sentra driving slowly as if searching for an address. Sunlight reflected in the windshield. I couldn't see the driver's face.

I pulled the Fury over and parked. The Sentra continued down the street and turned at the corner. False alarm. I was getting paranoid.

"Okay, come on, girl, we'll go home," I said. The Fury gave a choke, a gurgle and went dead. "Damn it, I just put in a new battery."

I got out and raised the hood, and when I did, the brown Sentra went by. From my hiding spot under the hood, I watched as the car paused by the house. I could see that the driver was tall and balding.

A friendly neighbor stopping by to borrow a cup of sugar? I didn't think so. *Come on, come on, get out of the car*, I thought. *Give me a chance to grab you.*

But after a few moments, he drove on. I ran down the sidewalk and managed to see the three letters of his license plate. I ran back to the Fury, but she still wouldn't start. I grabbed my cell phone, called Jordan and gave him the details, the man's description, his car, and the direction he was headed. Then I sat back and drummed a rhythm on the steering wheel.

Now how the hell did Wallace know that Margaret was staying there? Wouldn't I have noticed another car following her to the house?

A patrol car slid up beside the Fury, and the driver, a young policewoman, grinned at me.

"Thought that was you, Randall. It's hard to miss your great white whale of a car."

"Did you get the message about the Sentra?"

"I'm here to keep an eye on 1225. What's up?"

I explained about the mystery car and my suspicions.

She glanced at her computer. "Yeah, the alert just came in. NC plate, letters SBY. They're working on it. What are you doing here?"

"I wanted to make sure Margaret Layton was all right."

She took another look at the monitor. "She's staying with Patty and Debra Morenstein. Wallace is not likely to attack three women, is he?"

"I don't know and I don't want to find out."

"Well, looks like Officers Jacobs and Olsen are checking out the Sentra, and I'm staying put, so we're closing in on this guy." Another grin. "I'm sure at this point Jordan would tell you to go home."

I called the service station to come get the Fury, and then called Toad to see if he was anywhere in the neighborhood. He agreed to come by and give me a ride.

"Thought your old bucket was fixed," he said as I slid into Old Betsy.

"I thought so, too. She gave up at a good time, though. I would have been gone when Wallace came searching for Margaret. Jordan's bound to catch him this time."

"I hope so. Where to?"

It was time to put the fear of God—and me—into Stuart

King. "Super Food."

"Super Food? Is that the villain's hideout?"

"No, but it's where his faithful henchman works." His faithful, stupid, and maybe not so innocent henchman.

***

Super Food was one of those huge supermarkets that sold not only food but flowers, building supplies, pets, and lawn mowers. One of the employees directed me to the back of the store. I walked about five miles to a set of double doors marked "Employees Only" and pushed my way in. The supply room was also huge, masses of canned goods and toilet paper stacked high. There were dozens of little rooms and offices. I found Stuart's office by winding through the stacks to a narrow area between cartons of toys and a row of bicycles. The office backed up to the meat department and shared space with two enormous freezers. Stuart grinned when he saw me and motioned me over.

"Welcome to the bowels of Super Food. Have you come about a room at the Grace Street house?"

"It's a little more important than that."

"Sure. What's up?"

Looking at his pudgy, friendly face, I couldn't imagine him purposely sending Wallace out to kill. "Did you happen to get Margaret Layton's address or phone number for Wallace?"

He looked embarrassed. "Well, not exactly. I mean, I didn't ask her, but at the reunion, I heard her friend say she was staying with her on Sunnyside Avenue."

"You told Wallace this?"

He gulped. "Nothing's happened, has it?"

"No. Do me a favor, Stuart. If Wallace calls again or wants you to do anything, you have got to let me or the police know. You're better off not dealing with him anymore."

Stuart started to say "The police?" when one of the freezers kicked in, the motor chugging away like a freight train, and his voice was drowned out. He made a face and motioned for me to follow him to another area of the supply room where I could hear him. "The police? Why? What's going on?"

"There's a very good chance Bradley Wallace is the serial killer the police have been trying to catch for weeks."

Stuart paled. "A serial killer? A serial killer called *me?*"

"His usual accomplice was in jail."

Stuart took a step back. "Is that what the police think I am? This is horrible!"

"That's why you need to let me know if Wallace calls you, and if you can, get his phone number so the police can track him."

He nodded. "Okay." He looked at me with concern. "Do you think Wallace will come after me?"

"Well, you're not a woman and you're not blond."

He rubbed his bald head. "Yeah, I guess maybe I'm safe."

"I'll see if the police department can spare another officer for you."

"That would be great, Randall, thanks."

"One other thing, Stuart. You know where I live."

I let him work it out. It didn't take long. "Oh, I would never—you can't think that I would—"

"I'm working on this case with the police, and if Wallace hasn't figured that out by now, he will very soon. If anything happens to me or anyone in that house, you will definitely be considered an accessory and go to prison for a very long time."

"I swear to God I will not have anything else to do with Wallace."

*For now, I had to believe him*, I thought as I left the store. *But we do need to shadow Stuart. He might not give Wallace any more information, but Wallace might decide he was expendable.*

\*\*\*

When I called Jordan to ask about a tail for Stuart, he said the Sentra had been reported as stolen and they were still looking for it. Toad had waited in the Super Food parking lot and gave me a ride to the service station. This time, the problem was the starter. Once the Fury was on her wheels again and I'd left another small fortune with the mechanic, I drove home. Rufus and Angie, sitting on the front porch, lifted their cans of Mountain Dew in a welcoming salute.

"Hi, guys," I said. "What's the occasion?"

"Kary called to say there was a birthday party goin' on," Rufus said. "Must be a surprise party, 'cause no one's here."

"She went to pick up the cake. Come on in." I sent Kary a text to let her know I was home and so were Rufus and Angie.

Angie carried a small shiny gift bag. "We got Ellin a little something, even though we know she's a mite particular." She set the bag on the dining room table and took a seat on the island sofa. "How's life treatin' you, Randall? Found that killer yet?"

"No, but I'm getting closer." I hadn't seen Angie's picture or Rufus's in Ellin's yearbook. "Did either of you go to Parkland High School?"

""I went to East Ridge over near Pineville where I grew up," she said. "Rufe went to Ashe Valley."

"So you wouldn't know Bradley Wallace."

Rufus had gone into the kitchen to toss his soda can in the recycle bin. He returned with another Mountain Dew from the fridge. "Nope. Is he the guy?"

"Looks like it. I almost caught him today, but the Fury cut out on me."

"A heap of stirrin' and no biscuits."

"You could say that."

"Just did." He sat down beside Angie and popped open the can. "What about Cam? He still in low cotton?"

"Yes, Ellin's got him looking at houses today."

"That won't sit well."

About that time, Ellin and Camden returned from their day of Open House.

Camden unwound his scarf and hung it on the hall tree. "Honestly, Ellie, can't you tell how much more inviting this house is? When you walk in, don't you feel like you're home?"

"That's not really the point, is it?" she said. "This house is old and always needs some kind of repair. The houses we saw today are so beautiful and new and everything works."

"But I can fix anything here that breaks, and how in the world could we afford one of those new houses, anyway? This house is paid for."

"And always full of crazy people." She spared me a glance and acknowledged her two former tenants. "No offense, Randall, Rufus, Angie."

"Kary's not crazy, either," Camden said. "Honey, bottom line, we can't afford to move."

Ellin was glad to return to her favorite theme. "We would if you'd come on TV. Rufus, tell him he's being whatever it is you can say from your vast knowledge of Southern wisdom."

"So stubborn he'd argue with a fence post."

"Both of you stop," Camden said. "It's Ellie's birthday. Let's celebrate."

With excellent timing, Kary and Lottie arrived with the cake. We gathered around the table to sing "Happy Birthday," and Ellin blew out the candles. Angie's gift was a gold bracelet with a crescent moon charm. Ellin was truly pleased with it, so pleased she gave Angie a kiss on the cheek. She thanked Kary for the book. Lottie had bought an odd-looking ceramic animal that might have been a duck, and Ellin thanked her for that, too. Camden said he would save his gift for later. I didn't have a gift because I knew all Ellin wanted from me was for me to move out.

Everyone who has a party at 302 Grace knows the music will be traditional jazz. As the New Black Eagle Jazz Band zipped through "Tree Top Tall Papa," Kary cut the cake and gave everyone a slice. Camden put his arm around Ellin, and along with Rufus and Angie they listened with amusement as Lottie explained the plot of her newest mystery.

Kary handed me a plate full of cake and moved her chair closer to mine. "Anything happen on Sunnyside Avenue?"

"I almost had Wallace. Stuart inadvertently gave him the address of Margaret's friend, and I saw him drive by the house. The Fury chose that moment to give out, so I wasn't able to follow him."

"I still have my disguise if you want me to patrol the area."

"Thanks, but Jordan's got that covered." The song changed to John Gill's Original Sunset Five and their rendition of "Daddy,

Won't You Please Come Home?" I hadn't realized how many jazz tunes had "Daddy" or "Papa" in the title. I'd had a similar revelation with "Baby" songs when I was searching for Rufus's little Mary Rose.

I glanced at Kary's perfect face. She hadn't mentioned the baby again. *Adoption: Is It Right For You?* had been replaced by her stack of textbooks on guidance and counseling. I was probably better off not bringing up the subject. I still hoped I could be the one to find a solution.

The cake was a marble cake with chocolate frosting. I ate a couple of bites and set my fork aside. "Okay, you've known Camden longer than I have. Why is he always finding reasons not to be psychic? I thought we were done when he finally quit taking those pills. Can you explain why he refuses to accept what is so screamingly obvious to the rest of us."

Kary handed me another napkin. "Every now and then he gets into these moods. The fall was a convenient excuse."

"Do I need to call in the Snake Patrol?"

"That won't work. He's not afraid of snakes anymore."

"What else is he afraid of? Clowns? I could hire Stuart to jump out of a closet."

"He's accepted his talent, right? Just as you've accepted yours." She gave me a slightly modified Teacher Look. "You have, haven't you?"

There was only one right answer. "Yes, ma'am."

"Good. I've had enough nonsense from the two of you. I think we're well on our way to solving this case. Stuart King's not a threat and might still be really useful. We'll catch Mr. Clairol. You'll see."

Rufus and Angie spent the rest of the afternoon visiting. That evening, Camden took Ellin out for a special birthday dinner, and they returned in a better mood. By the time Kary and I went to bed, there was silence from the third floor, a good sign. I figured the quarrel had been successfully postponed for another day.

\*\*\*

Lindsey came in bright and clear that night.

*You're on the right track, Daddy.*

I hesitated to ask if she'd seen any of Wallace's other victims. "Have you seen a woman named Pauline Raterman?" I hoped that wherever Pauline Raterman was her head had been restored.

*Delores talks to the older folks, she said. I don't get to see everyone. Mostly kids like me. But I'll ask.*

"Thanks, baby."

*Cam will be all right.*

"Yes, he's doing okay."

*You are, too, Daddy. You'll figure all this out. You'll see.*

Now where had I heard that before?

\*\*\*

Monday morning I was at my desk hoping to hear from Wallace when Ellin marched in my office.

"I need to have a word with you."

Camden was in the backyard raking leaves. Kary was at school, and Lottie had gone to the grocery store. There was no one between me and a decidedly annoyed Mrs. Camden, who crossed her arms and let me have it.

"Randall, am I supposed to believe that Bradley Wallace is the serial killer and he's going to *call* you? Here at this house?"

Camden wouldn't have said anything. Kary wouldn't. Who did that leave? "Lottie spilled the beans, didn't she?" Again. I was going to have to have strong words with our resident stool pigeon.

"Not exactly. She was chattering away about the plot for her latest book. It seems her heroine, Dottie McVey, a retired school teacher, was helping Davidson Randolph on a serial killer case, and what a clever idea he'd come up with. Would you like to guess what this clever idea might be? Getting his young client's useless father, Arnold, and a reunion crasher named Stanley to lead them to the murderer, who would then call Davidson so he and the ever so charming Preston could go meet this villain face to face." She gave me a look that indicated she knew all. "Does any of this sound familiar to you? This killer's not dropping by to check out a room and move in, is he?"

If you only knew, I wanted to say. "Everything's under control, I promise. This is a good chance to catch Wallace. Jordan's got officers everywhere."

"You're just saying that to try to please me."

"Nope. I'd never try to please you. Look out the window if you don't believe me."

She glanced out the window. "What am I supposed to see?"

"That unmarked police car parked across the street."

You know that little blue part at the bottom of a candle flame where it's the hottest? Ellin's eyes went even bluer with rage. "And why would we need police protection? Is that killer meeting you *here*? Damn it, Randall!"

"No. He's not coming here. Do you honestly think I'd let someone like that anywhere near the house?"

"Didn't you see Wallace at the reunion? Why didn't you call the police then?"

"No, he sent a ringer in his place, the crasher Lottie told you about."

"Do you even know for certain he's the killer?"

"Yes, and I'm going to catch him. When you were in high school, he was crazy about Margaret Layton, and because she never gave him the time of day and his blond mother rejected him and ran off, he's decided to scalp all the blonds he can." Before she could reload, I said, "Do you remember a classmate of yours named Yvonne Thompson? I believe he murdered her, too."

This caught her attention. "Her murder was never solved."

"She was also blond."

She took a long seething moment. "How much of this does Cam know?"

"All of it."

I thought she might flame up again, but this time, her gaze was concerned. "Can you assure me that this killer won't come to the house?"

"I promise I won't let anything happen." The minute the words left my mouth, I felt a rush of unwanted emotion. I'd made a promise like this before.

Ellin's face showed a rare moment of sympathy and for another rare moment she didn't say anything. Then she said, "I do not appreciate being the last one to know about this. Why is Cam involved? Why are you involved? I thought Jordan didn't want you interfering with police work."

"This case was too important. We needed to cooperate. The minute we pinpoint this guy's location, we'll have him. There's nothing for you to worry about."

I'm not sure what she would've said next. I was saved by the ring of her cell phone. She marched off to the island where I could hear her firing off the rest of her anger at some hapless PSN employee.

Then I had a phone call. "Unknown" was on the Caller ID.

Wallace's voice was as dry and noncommittal as before. "Mr. Randall, I'd like to discuss this inheritance."

There was an odd wheezing sound in the background. Was he standing next to the railroad tracks? "How about we meet at Perkie's Coffee Shop near the park, say tomorrow at two o'clock?"

"No, I'll call back with the details," he said and ended the call.

Once again, I tried to reverse call, but Wallace must have bought a six-pack of burn phones. Other than the strange sound I'd heard, I had no clue.

Expecting Ellin to have caught Camden up in her own personal tornado and carried him off, I was surprised to see him still raking leaves in the backyard.

"Wallace just called," I said. "See if you can get anything off the phone."

He put down the rake and took my cell phone. He held it for a few minutes and then handed it back to me. "Sorry, nothing."

I didn't think that would work, but I had to let him try. "I'm not sure where he was, but it was very noisy. Sounded like that pitiful mini-fridge in the apartement where Allison McRay was killed."

"He wouldn't have gone back there."

"I don't think so, either."

"What did he say?"

"He's ready to meet, but he wants to name the time and place. He said he'd call back with details. I'll put him on speaker and maybe you can tell what that noise is."

We settled in my office to wait for the call. When Ellin screamed, we leaped up and ran to the kitchen. She pointed out the back window. "He was here! I saw him! Come on!"

"Ellie, no!" Camden said in alarm as she took off through the kitchen door.

We dashed out to the backyard and each took a different direction, Camden running after Ellin. I crashed through the hedge in time to see a figure running through the neighbors' back yard. "Over here!" I called.

I joined Camden and Ellin on the front sidewalk. "It wasn't Wallace," Camden said. "It was Tom. Ellie scared him when she screamed. I'd better go get him."

She made an exasperated sound. "Well, how was I supposed to know that? And who the hell is Tom?"

"A misunderstood werewolf," I said.

She gave me a look and went into the house.

That's when my phone rang. I answered. "Hello?"

The strange background noise continued to chug. "Mr. Randall," the calm voice said. "I'd like for us to meet at twelve fifty-five West Emerald, tomorrow at three." He hung up.

When Camden returned thirty minutes later, Tom followed cautiously and was finally coaxed up on the porch for a snack. I told Camden he'd missed the call.

"He wants to meet me at twelve fifty-five West Emerald tomorrow at three," I said.

Ellin came out and halted when she saw Tom. "What is that man doing here again? Why are you feeding him?"

"You remember me telling you about Tom," Camden said.

"He scared the life out of me. All this talk about a creep who cuts off women's hair, and then I see that bushy face looking in at me—this wouldn't happen if we lived in Starwood."

Camden gave me a weary look and tossed Tom another sandwich. "Maybe not."

"If you wouldn't feed him, he'd go away."

Tom ducked his head and made a growling sound.

"He says he's sorry," Camden said. "He didn't mean to frighten you. He saw the police car and didn't want to come in the front."

"Make him go away."

"Come on, Tom."

Camden started to walk off with Tom when my phone rang again.

"Wait," I said. "That might be Wallace."

But it was Stuart, his voice shaking. "Randall, Wallace just called me here at the store. He wants me to pretend to be him and meet you at the old deli on Emerald Street tomorrow at three."

"What did you tell him?"

"I told him the truth. I told him I couldn't get off work at three. He said thanks anyway and hung up."

"It's okay, Stuart. Good move."

"What if he finds out we know each other?" Stuart said. "He won't be happy about it."

"With any luck, he'll be in jail long before he figures that out. Don't worry. I don't think he'll try anything in the middle of Super Food."

Stuart laughed a nervous laugh. "Yeah, I guess you're right. Now that I know what he is, just hearing his voice gives me the willies."

"Me, too," I said, "but we'll catch him. He'll just have to find himself another go-between."

And I knew who that might be.

# Chapter Twenty-One

*"I've Got a Cross-Eyed Papa But He Looks Straight To Me"*

After a while, Camden came in and slumped down in the chair I have for clients. I hadn't heard a car drive up and recalled that the last time I saw Camden he and Tom were walking off towards Food Row.

"You help Tom catch a train out of town?" I asked.

"He decided to try the Salvation Army shelter on Shorter Street."

"Shorter? Did you two walk all the way over there?"

"Tom's used to walking long distances. I think it calmed him down."

"Then you walked all the way back? Why didn't you call? I could've swung around and picked you up."

"I needed to walk a long distance, too."

"Did it help?"

He leaned forward in the chair, his hands clasped. "You're not the only one Lindsey's trying to reform."

"Has she been giving you a hard time?"

"Yes. She gets that from you."

"What's she been telling you?"

"What I've known all along. If I have this talent, I ought to use it to help people."

"So no more pretending you're normal?"

He sat back and pushed his hair out of his eyes. "It wasn't all that great."

"Okay, partner." I explained about the meeting at three to-morrow and that Stuart was no longer involved with Wallace. "I thought murdering Pauline Raterman was Wallace's way of saying to Arliss keep quiet or your family's next."

"But Arliss doesn't care about Doreen or his wife."

"Right, but Arliss told me he'd seen the murder. So that's the hold Wallace has on him. Arliss didn't mention this little fact to Jordan."

"Seems to me that would be the hold Arliss has on Wallace."

"You'd think so."

"Maybe Wallace has threatened to kill someone Arliss does cares about."

I couldn't imagine Arliss having a significant other. "A girl-friend? Really?"

"You gave him a ride from the police station, right? Let me sit in your car."

Camden slid into the passenger's seat of the Fury and sat for a long time, carefully touching any surface Arliss might have come in contact with. "You took him to Meechum's bar."

"Yep. Got it in one."

"He was very anxious to get there."

"Well, he hadn't had a drink in a couple of days."

"That's part of it, but he needed to talk to somebody."

"A blond somebody?"

"I don't know."

"Worth a shot." I started the car. "Excellent butt-reading, by the way."

Camden's grin was reluctant, but at least it was a grin. "It's a gift."

\*\*\*

Many bars in Parkland were closed on Sundays. Meechum's wasn't one of them. It was small, dark, and grubby, with only one TV set with bad reception, three beat-up video game machines, and a gloomy corner where men and women sat scratching vainly at lottery tickets. The floor under them and the air around was filled with silvery flakes.

Arliss wasn't there. Camden and I found an empty table near the door. When the waitress approached, we both knew right away she was a contender for Arliss Padgett's Other Woman. Although I doubted blond was her original hair color, she was blond now, a brassy yellow-gold shade gathered in a pile of tight curls. She wore dark jeans and a white shirt, big gold hoop earrings, and a ring on each manicured finger, the fingernails a bright neon pink with silver edges. Her nametag said "Leyshelle."

She popped her gum. "What'll it be?"

I ordered a beer and a Coke. "We're looking for a friend of ours, Arliss Padgett."

"Oh, yeah? How do you guys know him?"

"We're old high school buddies in town for the reunion."

"You missed him there, then. He told me he didn't go."

"Yeah, we didn't see him there. Thought maybe we could get together here, talk about old times."

Her glance measured me. "Were you on the basketball team, too? He's told me about how he was their best shooter."

"We couldn't have done without him."

"Ain't he a caution? I'll be right back with your drinks."

As Leyshelle walked away, Camden said, "If she's Arliss's girlfriend, how did Wallace find out about her?"

"Maybe he comes to Meechum's, too. Now I'm wondering where Arliss is."

Leyshelle returned with the drinks. "Who gets the Coke?"

"Right here." Camden reached for the glass and purposely bumped her hand. "Whoops, sorry."

"No problem."

"Those are some beautiful rings you have."

"Thanks."

"May I?"

"Sure," she said.

He held her hand and admired the jewelry. "Very nice."

"The big one's from my ex."

He thanked her and let go. He gave me a slight nod.

"Leyshelle," I said, "there's another member of our class we're hoping to find, a fellow named Bradley Wallace. He's tall, thin, and bald. He might have come in with Arliss."

"Oh, yeah. He was in here the other day.  Him and Arliss was having a real serious-looking conversation, so after I brought their drinks, Arliss shooed me away. Talking about high school, I reckon."

I reckon it was exactly that. Talking about the reunion and how Arliss was to report on Margaret. And Wallace was getting a good look at Leyshelle.

"Has he been in lately?"

"Nah, just that one time. I asked Arliss who he was, and he said just a friend from high school, a team mate. He did look tall enough to play basketball." The bartender called for her to pick up another order. "Gotta go. I'll check back with you later."

Camden took a straw from the holder on the table. "She and Arliss are definitely an item."

"My mind will not go there."

He glanced over his shoulder at Leyshelle taking orders for three bikers at another table. "I'm a little worried about her."

"If Wallace attacks her, there goes his leverage."

"I think he's crazy enough not to care about that."

I took a sip of beer. "We're bound to catch him tomorrow."

Leyshelle returned. "Arliss is usually here by now."

He was off Plotting Evil Plans with Wallace. "That's okay. We'll try again later. If he comes in, tell him we said hi."

"Sure thing. Anybody need a refill?"

"No, thanks." I handed her enough for the drinks and a large tip.

She tucked the bills into her pocket. "Thanks."

We finished our drinks and went back to the Fury. "I didn't really want to see Arliss," I said. "Once a day is more than enough."

Camden hooked his seat belt. "I feel very uneasy about Leyshelle. I think we ought to call Jordan."

Jordan answered on the first ring. "Have you heard from Wallace?"

"Not yet, but Camden had a premonition about a blond waitress at Meechum's named Leyshelle, who is Arliss Padgett's girl-friend. She remembers seeing Wallace and Arliss together. It might be a good idea to have an officer keep an eye on her."

"Got it. No calls, though?"

"No, but it's a long time until tomorrow at three."

"Wallace may be on to us." Jordan's tone changed. "You two aren't hanging around Meechum's, are you?"

As we were already sitting in the car ready to drive home, I could truthfully say no. "Out running a few errands. We're headed back to Grace Street right now."

\*\*\*

I checked the recent calls on my phone. Two unfamiliar numbers that turned out to be telemarketers. Had Wallace decided three hundred thousand dollars wasn't enough to risk being discovered? Had he turned on Arliss, killed him, and left the city? Had he made a car out of hair and driven off into the sunset?

I heard Camden and Lottie talking in the island.

"I really wish I'd had more time to hear about all your adventures," Lottie said. "Kary said something about you being possessed by a dead songwriter. Is that true?"

When I had moved into 302 Grace a year ago, recovering a lost song book and solving a decades old mystery had been my first case. The composer of the songs hadn't let being dead stop him from hopping into Camden to express his views on how I handled the investigation.

"That's true," Camden said. "Although I don't remember a lot about it."

"She said another time she dressed up as a superhero and saved David who was attacked in tunnels under Parkland. That sounds amazing."

"That's true too. She provided an excellent distraction so Randall could get the drop on the bad guy."

"Then I suppose she really was a magician's assistant for another case?"

"Yes, and most recently, a Sixties Flower Child."

"My goodness, there's enough material here for a whole series."

"I'm sure Kary won't mind if you borrow a few ideas."

"I'm going to ask her right now."

Camden came to my door with a notepad and pen. "I'm making a list of the people to invite for Thanksgiving dinner. Think your mom would be available?"

"I'll call her and find out. Who else are you inviting?"

He sat down in the client's chair. "It's a pretty long list." He read off the names, which included his foster sister, Daisy, some of our neighbors, and all of our tenants, past and present.

"Are you inviting everyone who ever lived at 302 Grace?"

"Looks like it. Of course, some people might not be able to come."

"That's almost thirty people."

"I really want this to be a special Thanksgiving dinner. I want Ellie to see how wonderful this house can be, especially when it's full of people and food."

While I'd always celebrated Thanksgiving with a house full of people and food, Camden had missed a lot of holidays when he was traveling around the country. "I'm all for that."

Camden stood and put the notepad in his jeans pocket. "Sorry about being useless lately."

"Sorry I didn't have a couple of spare snakes."

"I'm going to deal with this."

Oh, ha, ha. "No, you're not. You're going to be as neurotic as ever. One day, pills. The next, falling off the roof. Can't wait to see what you'll try next."

There was a brief exchange of hand gestures, and we were done.

# Chapter Twenty-Two

*"You're Such a Cruel Papa To Me"*

Camden was getting out the leftover church ham and green beans when Lottie came in carrying a recyclable Super Food bag filled with groceries.

"Oh, I was planning to make supper tonight, Cam. I've got all the ingredients for my Super Deluxe Casserole."

Camden had no problem with that. He put the ham and beans back in the fridge. "The kitchen is yours."

"I can make as much as you want."

"Usually, Rufus and Angie come over on Monday night. If you count me, you, Randall, Kary, and possibly Ellie, I'd say make a big pile of food."

"No problem."

With Lottie stirring and frying, I held a meeting with my two partners in crime in my office to bring Kary up to speed on the case.

"First of all, you'll be glad to know Camden is psychic again."

She'd taken the chair, and Camden propped himself on the desk. She leaned over to poke his arm. "I knew it."

"This may be hard to believe, but Arliss Padgett has a girlfriend, a blond waitress at Meechum's. We're pretty sure that's how Wallace is keeping him in line."

"Then she's a target."

"I've already alerted Jordan."

"Okay, now what?"

"Now we wait until I meet Wallace tomorrow at three."

"Do you really think he'll show?"

"Camden?"

He shook his head. "I know I'm back online, but I can't tell if he'll be there."

"If he doesn't come, I'll have to think of something else, but I'm running out of ideas."

Cindy slid in the door and yowled at Camden. "Your food dish is empty again?" he said. "Okay, I'm coming."

As soon as he left, Kary said, "You know you can do this. Just channel your inner Davidson Randolph. 'Here's the dashing Davidson Randolph on the case, his brow furrowed like a trench, his dark hair gleaming like a new set of tires.'"

"Oh, I'll do you one better. 'As he leaned in for a kiss, Davidson couldn't help but admire Carrie Invers' luscious ruby lips, as red as the crust on a ketchup bottle lid.'"

She laughed. "But a lot more tasty."

\*\*\*

Ellin came home in time for supper and joined the crowd around the table. Lottie's casserole was a surprise, a big hit with everyone, a tasty combination of vegetables and strips of turkey over rice, seasoned with soy sauce and sesame oil.

"Hey, Lottie, pass me some more of that rice," Rufus called from across the table. "Mighty good food you got here."

I couldn't resist. "How good?"

"So good if you put it on top of your head, your tongue would slap your brains out trying to get to it."

"Can't stump you, Rufus."

"Naw, don't even try." He pointed his fork at Lottie. "You can come over to our place and cook for me and Angie any time."

There was another round of compliments to the chef, and then the conversation changed to questions about Rufus and Angie's new home, followed by congratulations to Lottie and her book covers, and then Kary mentioned her plans for the desserts she wanted to make for Thanksgiving.

"Along with pumpkin pie, I thought coconut cake and cherry pie would be good, but I'm open to any other ideas."

No one had any issues with coconut cake and cherry pie.

"There'd better be leftovers," Rufus said, and Kary assured him they'd make extras.

Into this pleasant scene came a loud knocking and then Doreen burst in. "Randall! Do you know what that low life has done? He's got the nerve to have this tarted up b—" She stopped dead still. "Oh! Oh, sorry! Didn't know you was—sorry, everyone! I'd better go."

I hopped up and escorted her to my office. "No, it's okay. Come have a seat in here. What's the matter?"

She was trying not to cry. "I didn't mean to bust in like that and ruin your dinner."

"It's okay, Doreen. Tell me what's wrong." I closed the door and took my seat behind the desk. I handed her a tissue. "Is this about Leyshelle?"

"Uh-huh." She blew her nose. "I went outside on break to talk to one of the other girls who was having a cigarette and seen 'em together outside of the drug store. I got so mad, I run over there and gave him what for."

I'd heard Rufus use "what for" and knew it meant giving someone a big piece of your mind. "I'm sure that upset you, but you don't want him in your life anymore, do you?"

"No, but it made me so mad." She gulped back another sob. "When I seen him, I thought for a moment he'd come by to see me. I mean the drug store's right across the street, and he could've been coming over to the Quik-Fry. Then I saw that woman, and I knew he'd really forgotten Mama and me." She wiped the last tears away and fixed me with a suspicious gaze. "How'd you know her name?"

"Camden and I talked to her earlier today at Meechum's."

"How come?"

"Did you ask your mother if she knew Bradley Wallace or ever heard your dad mention him?"

"Yes, and she said she'd never heard of him, so I didn't figure

I needed to call you about that."

"Camden and I thought Leyshelle might know Wallace."

"Was you going to tell me about her?"

"We didn't think that was necessary."

"You was probably right. If I'd known about her, I would've gone to that bar and pulled out all her tacky bleached hair."

"Doreen."

She balled up the tissue and threw it in the trashcan. She caught my expression, hunched one thin shoulder, and turned away peevishly. "Well, I would've."

"What happened when you gave Arliss what for?"

"That woman says, 'Who's this?' and he says, 'Ain't nobody important,' and I says, 'I'm his daughter. Who are you, you tramp?' and he says, 'Go away, girl,' and gave me a shove. I lit into him best I could, but he kept pushing me away until him and that woman got into her car. Then it was time for me to go back to work." Laughter from the dining room made her glance toward the door. "Guess I should've called, but I was so mad."

She'd deflated and looked worn out. I handed her another tissue. "Would you like some dinner?"

"No, thanks. I sure could use a ride home, though, if you don't mind."

On the way to the trailer park, Doreen was quiet. I kept looking at her sharp profile, so different from Lindsey's soft little face. I thought of all the advantages I'd given my daughter and how Doreen had to scrape along on her own. What if I'd died in that crash and Barbara and Lindsey had been left alone? It didn't seem likely, but what if they'd ended up in a dismal trailer park?

I pulled up beside Doreen's trailer. Before she got out, she asked, "Any news about a better job?"

"I'm working on it. I'll find something for you, I promise."

She grimaced as if she'd heard people promise things many times and never come through, which was probably true for her. "It's no big deal if you can't, Randall. I never seem to have much luck anyways."

I was not going to let her give up. "Doreen, you remember when you came to ask me to find your father?"

"I remember. You didn't want to do it."

"You asked to be my last deadbeat dad case."

"Thought at least I'd give it a try."

"I'm glad you did. I've done a lot of thinking since then, and I've decided I don't want to give up, no matter what the case involves."

She squinted her eyes in disbelief. "What made you change your mind?"

"You did." As well as a certain little girl who also didn't want me to give up.

Now her eyes were wide. "No foolin'?"

"You told me 'If you're good at something, you stick to it.'" I offered her my hand. "Neither one of us is allowed to feel sorry for themselves anymore, okay?"

She shook my hand. "Okay, then."

I waited until she was safely inside the trailer and drove back to the house. Rufus's blue bigfoot truck was still parked out front, and there was plenty of casserole left.

"What was all that ruckus about?" Rufus asked as I took my place at the table. He and Angie were on what must have been their third helping. Amazingly, Ellin was still eating and not on the phone to the network. Lottie and Kary were in the kitchen hunting in the cabinets for the dishes they'd need for the desserts, and Camden was pouring more tea in everyone's glasses.

"Doreen needed a ride home," I said.

Rufus took a big gulp of tea. "Sounds like she got into an altercation."

I paused in the act of scooping more rice. "'Altercation.' Good one."

"Fancy-ass word for ruckus. Who's the other woman?"

"A waitress at Meechum's."

"Have to be mighty drunk to take up with Arliss."

I couldn't let another opportunity pass. "How drunk?"

"Drunk as a skunk."

"I didn't think skunks could get drunk."

"Why you think they smell so bad?"

Camden sat down and reached for the sugar bowl. "Is Doreen

okay?"

"Yes. She said her mother didn't know anything about Wallace, though."

"Somebody keepin' an eye on Leyshelle?" Rufus asked.

"Somebody's keeping an eye on everyone," I said. "Pretty soon Jordan's going to be out of officers."

"Pretty soon you're gonna catch this guy."

"Are you sure about that?" I asked, knowing he'd have just the right reply.

"As sure as life is short and full of blisters."

# Chapter Twenty-Three

*"Sweet Papa Will be Gone"*

Rufus and Angie were happy to take the leftover casserole home and roared off in the bigfoot truck. Kary had an idea for a PSN show, and she and Ellin went upstairs to discuss it. Camden washed the dishes while I channel-surfed to find a reasonably bad science fiction movie for our evening entertainment. I thought everyone was safe for the night until Camden came to the island, eyes wide.

"Call Jordan. Something about Leyshelle."

"Good God, she's not dead, is she?"

"Call him now."

I did. "Jordan, Camden says Leyshelle might be in danger."

"Not anymore," he said. "We're at her house. She was attacked a few minutes ago. Fortunately for her, we had an officer on duty, and a neighbor who was coming in from work helped chase off her assailant. She's shaken up, but she's going to be all right."

"Did she get a good look at her attacker? Was it Wallace?"

"She was attacked from behind. Says someone grabbed her by the hair, and when she screamed and fought back, that's when the neighbor ran over."

"Did the neighbor give you a description? What about your officer?"

"Said it was too dark. They chased him, but he got away." I heard voices in the background and a distant siren. "We're canvassing the neighborhood, and Miss Grant's on her way to the hospital. Do not, I repeat, do not talk to her or anyone else Arliss Padgett is involved with. It's obvious Wallace is watching him, and we don't need any more targets."

He ended the call. Camden's gaze was intent. "She's all right, then?"

"Yes, thanks to the police and a neighbor. Jordan's warned us off, as usual, but I'm not going to make any more trouble for Leyshelle."

"Does Jordan think it was Wallace?"

"Too dark to tell, he said." I had a sudden sinking feeling. "We need to talk to Stuart."

"Randall, it's not Stuart."

"Let's go see." I couldn't interview Leyshelle, but I sure as hell could ride by Super Food and look for a brown van.

Camden was annoyed by my suspicions. "You wanted me to be psychic and now you won't believe me."

"A short trip to the grocery store will solve this problem."

We drove to Super Food and circled the parking lot until we saw Stuart's brown Chevy van.

"There," Camden said. "Mystery solved."

"He could've switched cars." I parked the Fury. "I have a sudden urge for some chips and dip."

The store wasn't crowded at nine o'clock, and it was easy to find Stuart up front near the office area chatting with some of his co-workers.

"Oh, hi, guys," he said. "What's up?"

"Out for a drive," I said. "Point me to the potato chips."

"Aisle six. Cam, I want you to meet my friends. The people at the reunion said you were psychic." He introduced Camden to his co-workers. "I know the store is haunted. Tell him about all the ghostly things that have been going on around here, everybody. Stuff's been moved around and some things have been stolen."

Perfect. While I wandered off in search of snacks, Camden could shake everyone's hand and learn exactly what Stuart had been up to. He might even catch their ghost. I bought a bag of chips and came back to the group.

"So what's the verdict?" I asked. "Is it a poltergeist? The ghost of a disgruntled shopper?"

"I'm getting a strange sort of feeling, but there hasn't been any spirit activity," Camden said. "It's most likely a shoplifter."

Stuart looked disappointed, and his friends chuckled. "We didn't really think there was anything to it," one said.

We said good-by to Stuart and friends and went back to the Fury.

"Stuart's been here checking on his work schedule and telling his co-workers ghost stories," Camden said. "That's all. You have to admit he does not fit the profile of criminal mastermind."

"I yield to your superior psychic insight." I offered him the bag. "Chip?"

"Hand them over."

***

Tuesday morning seemed to go on forever. Ellin went to the PSN. Kary went to school. I continued my job search for Doreen, but my mind kept circling around to three o'clock. Would Wallace show? Would Jordan and I be able to catch this killer and put an end to his reign of terror? Reign of terror? Being around Lottie was a bad influence on me. She'd bounded in during breakfast to grab a bagel and rush back to *Death in Disguise*. I expected her at my door any moment with the next chapter clutched in her hot little hand. I wondered if Davidson Randolph could've done better with this case.

Half-way through the morning, I called Jordan to see if Arliss had led the police to Wallace. No luck.

"How are they getting past you?" I asked.

"Parkland's a big city, and our resources are stretched thin. Sooner or later they're going to make a mistake."

I was concerned Wallace had staked out the Quik-Fry and that Doreen was going to be his next victim. "You've got somebody at the Quik-Fry, right?"

"Part of that stretched thin I just mentioned."

"Did Leyshelle remember anything else about her attacker?"

"No, and we've got an officer with her, too. Settle down. We've got this under control."

Maybe Jordan thought things were under control, but I still couldn't shake the feeling I'd overlooked something.

\*\*\*

Jordan called back at two thirty. "I'll be stationed in an unmarked car where I can see you. Keep Wallace occupied and we'll surround him."

But when I arrived at twelve fifty-five West Emerald at three o'clock, there was Arliss Padgett. I'd parked one street over so the Fury wouldn't be recognized and walked to the meeting place. From here I could see Jordan's car at the corner.

Arliss gave me a sour grin. "Ain't this a treat?"

"Wallace couldn't make it?"

"Seems he's right anxious to get out of town. Can't imagine why."

"Wouldn't have anything to do with your girlfriend Leyshelle, would it?"

His face twisted into an angry snarl. "That's all your fault, you and your friend coming around asking her questions about me, getting her all suspicious. I told Wallace she didn't know nothing, but he went after her all the same."

"Gives you some idea of the type of lunatic you're dealing with. Tell me where he is and help me get him."

"Hell, I don't know. He finds me. And even if I knew, I wouldn't tell you, you and your stupid inheritance scam. I told him he wasn't getting no money from you 'cause you was the smartass detective what got me in trouble. Let's just say he wasn't too happy about that."

A few warning bells went off. What else had Arliss told Wallace? "Help me catch him and you won't have to worry about him threatening your girlfriend anymore."

But Arliss was too afraid of Wallace to consider double-crossing him. He glanced around nervously. "You got Finley hiding in the bushes somewhere, I'll bet."

"If you're scared of Wallace, I can take you to the police station."

"Cops don't care what happens to me."

"How about if I take you to the hospital? You can stay with Leyshelle. There's an officer guarding her door."

This appealed to him, but his eyes shifted warily. "Can you guarantee I'll be safe?"

"Depends on how much you cooperate."

"Forget it." Abruptly his scowl changed to a smirk. "Actually, I got one more thing to tell you. You know, I been to your house that time you and Doreen set a trap for me. I mighta mentioned to Wallace about all them pretty blonds that live there."

Now the warning bells were full-blown sirens. Had Wallace sent Arliss Padgett as a diversion while he made his way to Grace Street? The cold feeling in my spine traveled all the way through my body. Kary was at home making desserts. I didn't want to take the chance that Arliss was lying. I grabbed him by the arm and propelled him toward Jordan's car. Jordan and another officer jumped out, and I shoved Arliss toward them.

"Wallace may be at my house."

I didn't waste another second. I ran back to the Fury and made a wild U turn to head for home. On the way, I called Kary and was vastly relieved when she answered.

"Hi, David."

I tried to keep my voice calm. "How are those desserts coming along?"

"Oh, just fine."

"Do me a favor and make sure all the doors are locked."

"What's wrong?"

"I'll be there in a few minutes."

I drove home as fast as I could and dashed into the house. Kary and Lottie were in the kitchen. Lottie almost dropped a can of cherry pie filling.

"My goodness! You startled me."

Kary's hands were white with flour. "What's the matter?"

I knew Doreen was all right at the Quik-Fry. I couldn't think for a minute, and then remembered there was another blond. But she'd be at the PSN, wouldn't she? I'd better check. As I scrolled down to find Ellin's number, I said, "I didn't want to alarm you, but Mr. Clairol might be in the neighborhood. Arliss was kind enough to give him our address."

My phone rang and Jordan's anxious voice said, "We're on the way."

"It's okay," I said. "He's not in the house. But he may still be around."

"We'll be there in a few minutes."

"Was that Jordan?" Kary asked. "I locked all the doors and windows. Wallace won't get in."

Camden rarely remembered to have his cell phone on, but Ellin was practically fused to hers. Now there was no answer. "I'm calling Ellin, but she's not answering. She must be filming something."

"Oh, she came home early to help with the desserts."

"What?" This was such un-Ellin like behavior my mind went blank.

"We were talking about it earlier, and she said she'd like to help. We ran out of coconut, so she and Cam went to get some more."

"Where did they go? Super Food?"

"Yes. About half an hour ago. What's wrong?"

My mind went into overdrive. What a great time for Ellin to decide to become domestic. Then a thought hit me like a brick. Super Food. My God. That strange chugging wheezing sound I'd heard in the background when Wallace called. The freezers in the back. A warren of little rooms. The perfect place for a psycho like Wallace to have a hideout. And hadn't Stuart said the store was haunted? Those noises employees reported hearing—could that have been Wallace creeping around?

"I'll be right back."

I hurried out to the Fury, turned to open the door, and something hit me hard on my back and my knees buckled. *Wallace! I thought. I'm too late. He's here.* I hit the ground, instinctively rolling to avoid another blow, which was good, because when I looked up, my stupid overgrown stalker Garrett Henderson was grinning and swinging a baseball bat. Now which was worse, a direct blow to the head, or a smashed arm from trying to deflect the blow?

Fortunately, I didn't have to make that choice. A large shape cannonballed out of the shrubbery, tackled Henderson and flung him down, then snatched the bat and clubbed him into silence. I got up quickly, ready to run from this new threat, and recognized my rescuer. Dark bead eyes gleamed furiously in a furry face.

"Thanks, Tom."

He growled and threatened the flattened Pumpkin Man with the bat.

"No, don't hit him again," I said. "You got him."

Another growl.

"Okay, you stay here, and if this guy tries anything, you have my permission to hit him again. Guard the house. Don't let anyone get in." Good dog!

Wincing, I got in the car. Of course this time the Fury wouldn't start. I gave the steering wheel an angry smack and ran back into the house.

"Kary, I need to use your car."

She'd already washed her hands and put on her coat. "I'm coming with you."

"Me, too," Lottie said.

"No. God, no. Both of you stay here. Call Jordan and tell him to meet me at Super Food."

Lottie took out her phone. "I can do that."

"You two stay here."

Kary always left her keys next to her pocketbook on the seat of the hall tree. I grabbed the keys. I thought I could outrun her, but Henderson's love tap had taken some of my steam. By the time I'd wedged myself into Turbo, her neon green Ford Festiva, she slid into the passenger's seat and Lottie hopped into the back.

"Cam and Ellin are in danger, aren't they?" Kary said. "We're coming with you."

There wasn't time to argue. On the way to Super Food, I explained what was going on. "I think Wallace has been hiding out in the store. Arliss came in Wallace's place to keep me and Jordan occupied."

"But Cam's with Ellin."

"And just about as blond as possible. All the more reason to make sure they're okay."

"David, do you know how many people shop Super Food on Sunday afternoon? Wallace won't be able to do anything in that kind of crowd."

"Yeah, but Stuart showed me lots of storage rooms in the back." We swung into the grocery store parking lot, and I slid the Festiva into the first empty spot I found. I switched Turbo off. "Stay in the car."

"No."

"Kary, please. This guy is after blonds. I mean it. Wait here."

"I'm coming with you," she said. "Come on, Lottie."

I couldn't convince them to stay put. We ran across the parking lot and into the store. Kary was right about the crowd. Dozens of people crowded the aisles of Super Food. This gave me the chance to push past them and leave a protesting Kary and Lottie tangled in the middle of two women blocking the soup aisle. I hurried to the back of the store and smacked open the silver double doors that led to the rear. Workers gave me curious glances as I passed them.

I jogged past Stuart's office and on to the storage rooms and started my search. There were dozens of storage rooms. Wallace could be anywhere. With each door I opened, I felt my stomach tense, expecting to find Ellin's dead body with a peeled head.

When I finally found what I was looking for, the sight was pretty ghastly, but no one had been scalped yet. Camden was sprawled unconscious in one corner. Mr. Clairol sat in the center of the room, Ellin unconscious at his feet. He was braiding a long rope of blond hair. God. I didn't want to think what another blow had done to Camden. I didn't want to imagine how he'd survive if Ellin was dead.

The serial nutball rolled his narrow eyes my way. He was tall and pale, his almost bald head gleaming in the faint light. He wore thin blue plastic gloves. "You stay right there. I'm finished."

"You sure are," I said. "Did you kill them?"

He glanced scornfully at Ellin. "Not yet." My heart settled somewhere near its original home. "I only needed a little more, but her hair is too short." A second scornful glance at Camden. "His is nice, but it's too short, too." He held up his rope. "This will have to do."

"If you can't use them, let me get them out of your way," I said. "Then you can finish in peace."

He considered my offer. "No." He rubbed his jaw. "She hit me. She's going first."

I had to attempt a rescue. "That's a very fine rope you've got there. Mind if I have a look?"

"A look?"

I took a cautious step forward. "You went to a lot of trouble to make it. Looks pretty good from here."

"It is," he said. "Made from the finest human hair."

I took another step. "Really? That's interesting. I didn't know human hair was that strong."

"I prefer women's hair." He inclined his head toward Camden. "But his is a very nice color. Very soft."

"Like Margaret's."

His eyes brightened. "Why, yes. Yes, it is. You know, she never let me touch hers. Then she cut it all off."

"That's too bad." Another step and I'd be close enough to grab the creep.

"I wouldn't have hurt her. My hands were always clean. But she never even turned around."

One more step. That's when I saw the long silver knife in his hand.

"Stay back! I'll kill them! I'll kill all of you!"

I stepped back. "Okay, okay, take it easy."

He reached over to grab Ellin's hair, but then his mouth dropped open. I turned to see what had caught his eye.

Kary came towards him, swinging her long silky hair. "Hey, there, killer," she said. "Here's what you really want."

Wallace looked stunned. Kary ran her hands through her hair, lifting it high so the strands slid slowly down like syrup. He forgot Ellin and Camden. His eyes focused on Kary's hair. He licked his lips.

"Come on, big boy," she said. "You don't want Ellin's puny little curls when you could have *this*."

I edged around and pulled Ellin over to the corner where Camden lay. Now I had both of them behind me while Wallace continued to drool over Kary. If she kept Wallace mesmerized long enough, I could make a try for his knife. Wallace was entranced. He dropped his rope and reached out his long fingers. Kary danced out of reach, teasing.

"Who are you?" he said. "Who are you?"

"Who do you want me to be? Margaret? I can be Margaret. You can finally touch her hair."

Wallace lunged faster than I could reach him, and for a few heart-stopping moments, I thought he'd grab Kary. Just as his fingers brushed her head, a furious voice boomed from the doorway.

"Bradley Ambrose Wallace! You put that knife down right now, young man!"

He gasped, stunned, and stared at Lottie. I don't know how she appeared to him. Perhaps for a moment he thought she was the verbally abusive mother who left him. At any rate, her stern Teacher Look and stiff posture, arms crossed, lips pursed, and eyebrows lowered was enough to make him drop his knife. Before he came out of his stupor, I kicked the knife away, snatched up the long braid, and lassoed him. He screamed and clawed, yanking a few strands free, but I wrapped the hair rope around his arms, pulled his elbows back and threw him to the ground. Kary planted her foot down hard on his back while I double knotted the rope.

"You're right," I said, out of breath. "This is a good strong rope."

He yowled and rolled on the floor, but the rope held and so did Kary's foot. His angry screams brought workers running. They piled up in the doorway, all talking at once. I called them over.

"Guys, come in here and sit on this man while I call nine-one-one."

A few of the braver souls plopped down on top of Wallace. Kary and Lottie ran to Camden as he groaned and sat up. He saw Ellin and completely freaked out. "Oh, God, oh, God." He held her in his arms, entreating her to wake up, to say something.

I found a strong pulse in her wrist. "Take it easy. I didn't give this jerk time to do anything."

"I couldn't stop him. I beat the hell out of him, and he kept coming." He stroked Ellin's hair, his hand trembling. "Ellie, please. Please wake up."

"She'll be all right," Kary said. "Are you okay?"

He looked at her as if seeing her for the first time. "What are you doing here?" Then he saw Lottie. "What's Lottie doing here?"

Kary gave him a reassuring hug. "Well, we finished making the desserts and decided to come to the rescue."

By the time the police and the ambulance arrived, Ellin had regained consciousness, which is a shame, because she's so quiet and beautiful when she's asleep. The EMS team had to give Camden oxygen. He was hyperventilating really well by then. With both of them safely packed away in the ambulance, and Mr. Clairol, now foaming at the mouth, safely packed away in a squad car, I had time to properly thank my partner.

Lottie had insisted on going with Camden and Ellin, which left me with Kary and a few dozen stunned Super Food employees.

Kary wound her arms around my neck. "Admit it. You need me."

"I've always said that. I don't want you putting yourself in danger."

"But you needed a distraction. Don't tell me you didn't."

"It was perfect. Thank you. But don't make a habit of it. Not all serial killers are going to be dazzled by your hair." I gave her a kiss and held her at arms' length. "That's as grateful as I can be right now. We need to go by the hospital and check on Camden and Ellin, and then go to the police station and tell Jordan what happened and more than likely fill out a long report."

"And collect a reward?"

"That's highly likely." I gestured to the rest of the store clerks who were still standing in the doorway, open-mouthed at the sight of her. "I think if you play your cards right, you can have free groceries for life."

# Chapter Twenty-Four

### *"My Heart Belongs to Daddy"*

By the time Kary and I finished at the police station, Camden and Ellin had been checked over and sent home. When we arrived, Ellin was asleep on the sofa, Camden hovering. Lottie and Stuart were pacing and trying not to run into each other.

"I had to come," Stuart said. "I had to make sure everyone was all right."

"How is she?" I asked Camden.

"Okay." He sat down beside her and held her hand. The doctors must have given him a big dose of something, because he was calm. "She's okay."

Kary gave him a hug. "She'll be okay. How are you doing?"

"I'm fine, thanks."

"I guess I'd better finish those desserts in case anyone feels like going to church tonight. Come on, Lottie."

"This was the most exciting thing that's ever happened to me," Lottie said. "I can't believe we caught a serial killer. It's like real life."

"It is real life," I said. Scary, heart-stopping, could have gone wrong in so many ways real life. "That was inspired what you did, Lottie. You really saved the day."

She blushed. "I remembered how his mother treated him. Poor fellow. He didn't stand a chance, did he? Imagine being verbally abused and then abandoned by your own mother."

Camden and I exchanged a glance. He'd been abandoned, too, but obviously he'd learned to handle his real life.

Lottie continued. "And that was so sad about that young girl he killed in high school. Didn't Jordan Finley say the thought of the reunion might have triggered Wallace?"

"Yes, and he's going to be put away for a long time," I said. "Arliss will also be spending some time for his part in all this."

"You pressed assault charges against Henderson the Pumpkin Man, too, didn't you?" Kary asked.

I rubbed my back which was fortunately bruised, not broken. "Yes, the jail is full."

Lottie had more to say about her adventure. "All this is going to be the basis for my next book: *Chain of Terror.*"

I had to ask. "Why *Chain of Terror*?"

She gave me her usual I Can't Believe You're So Dim look. "The crime happened in a Super Food. Super Food is a chain. A chain of grocery stores."

"You can explain in detail later." I wanted to hear what had happened when Ellin and Camden went to the store.

"We needed more coconut," Camden said. "We were near the back of the store when I got the feeling something was wrong. It was the same feeling I had when Stuart asked me to look for the ghost he thought was haunting the store. I also saw Ellie in danger, so I told her to stay where she was, I'd be right back, but she came with me. That's when Wallace grabbed her. Before I knew it, he'd hauled us both to the other room. He remembered Ellie from high school and was furious she'd cut her hair, too."

"I can't believe it," Stuart said, still pacing. "I can't believe something like this would happen in the store! You should've called me for help before you went back there, Cam."

"I'll remember that next time." He put his head in his hands. "God, I am so tired."

"What did the doctor say?" I asked.

"They told me to take it easy. I told them that's all I've been doing this month."

I went to the kitchen and found the box of Pop-Tarts. I didn't have to cook them. Camden will eat them raw. He'll eat them after they've been sitting out on the drain board for a few days. Two of these and a large glass of tea and he was more coherent. I got myself a beer and Kary a Diet Coke. I sat back in the blue armchair. Lottie had already hurried upstairs to start *Chain of Terror*, and Stuart finally settled in another chair.

"I don't know if this is really a good time," he said timidly, "but is there a room available here yet?"

Camden gave a slight laugh. "I think we can find something for you, Stuart."

"I mean, I'll understand if having me around brings back bad memories or something."

"Trust me," he said. "I have bad memories like you wouldn't believe."

"Oh, yeah, the psychic thing."

"That's one way to put it," I said. "And now you know the store's not haunted." Thinking of the store made me think of something else. "Stuart, are there any job openings at Super Food?"

"We're always looking for cashiers," he said.

"I may send someone your way."

"Sure. I'd be glad to help."

Camden leaned back on the sofa. "They found out something else at the hospital, Randall."

"You're growing that third eye you've always wanted."

"Ellie's pregnant with baby number one. It's a girl."

I lifted my beer can in salute. "Congratulations."

"That's wonderful," Kary said.

He gazed fondly at Ellin. "She's going to be as beautiful as her mother."

"Is the baby going to be psychic?"

"Oh, yes. Very much so. They all are."

We all sat in silence for a while. I thought of the sheer thrill of catching that madman, of rescuing my friends, of solving the crime. I thought of Jordan's look of admiration, something I didn't often see.

"Well," Kary said. "If everyone's all right, I'll see about the cake." As she passed my chair, she put her hand on my arm and leaned in. "I knew you could do it. I knew you could save them."

"Thanks," I said.

Now her beam was full of satisfaction. "With my help, of course."

***

Doreen stopped by the next morning with good news. She'd been hired by Super Food. The cashier's job fit Doreen's mathematical talents, and Stuart had helped her with the application.

"That's great, Doreen, congratulations," I said.

"You done it again, Randall," she said, grinning. "Found what I wanted."

"We'd like you and your mother to come to Thanksgiving dinner," Camden said.

"Thanks, I will." She leaned forward. "Can I ast you something? Will you tell my fortune? Not the bad parts. Just tell me if anything good's gonna happen soon."

"Okay." He took her skinny little hand. Doreen closed her eyes tight as if afraid of disturbing the vibes. After a moment, Camden let go of her hand. Her eyes flew open.

"You done already? What did you see?"

I know Camden well enough to tell when something's wrong, but all Doreen saw was a slight smile.

"I won't lie to you," he said. "Your life's going to be pretty hard. But it won't be long before you have some peace and quiet."

"Will I get married?"

"Yes," he said, which delighted her.

"Who's it gonna be? No, don't tell me. I like surprises. Do I have any kids? No, don't tell me that, either. It's enough to know I got a future, anyways." She straightened the nametag on her Super Food apron. "Least I got me a proper job. Better get going, too, if I want to keep it." She hesitated and then gave Camden a quick kiss on the cheek. "Thanks, Cam."

She picked up her saddlebag and hurried out. "How long does she have?" I asked.

"Four years," he said with difficulty. "Her husband kills her. Domestic dispute, Jordan calls it."

"Any way we can prevent that from happening?"

"It's what I see for her now. It could change, but it doesn't seem likely. Unless somebody breaks the pattern, people from abusive situations keep on finding abuse."

Not on my watch. "I won't let that happen," I said.

\*\*\*

Camden tells me the two things people want most to hear from departed loved ones are "It wasn't your fault" and "I'm proud of you." I always thought it was the parent's job to make sure the child knew how proud her father was of her, but my relationship with Lindsey had reversed that. More than anything, I wanted her to be proud of me.

The dream that night was fleeting, but I saw my little daughter standing at the edge of the playground. She was holding hands with Yvonne Thompson. She smiled her heartbreakingly sweet smile.

*I knew you would help that girl, Daddy. I knew you would do your best.*

I didn't have a chance to reply before someone called to her from the playground and the dream faded. But I had my answer.

\*\*\*

Everyone on Camden's Thanksgiving dinner list was able to come, so we had a house full of laughter and the tempting smells of roast turkey, savory dressing, fresh rolls, and two kinds of pie, apple and pumpkin. Everyone he'd invited had been able to come, so we had people around the dining room table, at the kitchen counter, on the window seat, and all over the island. Our actor friends Leo Pierson and his girlfriend Francine started the evening off with some dramatic recitations from Shakespeare. Lottie read a chapter from *The Raging Rapids* to stifled laughter and a round of applause. Then Kary played and Camden sang "We Gather Together" and "Come, Ye Thankful People, Come."

Ellin set an extra stack of napkins on the table. "It's good to hear him singing again."

I hadn't had a chance to ask her how she felt about being with child. "Are you okay about baby number one?"

Her expression gave nothing away. "We'll see."

My mother, fresh in from Bermuda and resplendent in her customary leopard print blouse, red leather skirt, and strings of pearls, had to hear all about my latest adventure.

"A serial killer with a hair fetish, Davey? What happened to all the ordinary murders? I hope this isn't a sign that crime in Parkland is going to get wilder. I thought all that business with the magicians was crazy, and then that cursed dragonfly, and now this."

"I'll be ready for whatever happens."

She gave my cheek a pat. "I know you will. Let's see, I've met all the people from the Psychic Service Network, and of course I know Jordan and Rufus and Angie. Who's the jolly fellow who brought all the food?"

Stuart provided a full Thanksgiving feast: turkey, dressing, cranberry sauce, sweet potatoes, the works, and a few guests brought special dishes and desserts, so there was plenty to eat. "Stuart King, our newest boarder. I'll have to show you his oversized animal costumes."

"Really? That sounds kinky. Now, I know the dark-haired woman is Denise, Camden's birth mother, and the older lady is his foster sister Daisy. Who is the woman sitting by Angie?"

Doreen's mother Hazel was chomping away at the sweet potatoes as if she hadn't eaten in days. "Hazel Padgett, my client Doreen's mother."

"Doreen's the tough-looking little girl?"

"Yes, and she is tough."

"I suppose she has to be. It looks like she and her mother have had a hard life."

A life I hoped to make better.

When Doreen came into the kitchen to help me slice the pumpkin pie, I had a chance to talk with her. "About what Camden told you. Since he fell off the roof, he's been all screwed up. I wouldn't put too much faith in his predictions."

She looked disappointed. "You mean I ain't getting married?"

"You know," I said, "sometimes I have psychic visions, too,

and I see a better future for you if you go in your own direction. I mean, look how your mother's marriage turned out. You don't have to get married."

She looked over at her worn mother, who was working her way through a plate filled with mashed potatoes and dressing. "Maybe. She once told me she wanted to be an actress, but then she met Padgett, and that took care of that."

Even though it was hard to imagine now, if Hazel Padgett had looked like Doreen when she was young, she might have been able to fulfill her dream.

"Your mom would want you to have a better life."

"Yeah, it's something to think about."

With so many people, the kitchen garbage can was soon full. I took one load of garbage out the back door and put it in the larger can. I glanced back at the warm golden squares of the windows and remembered what Camden had said. *Everything I care about is in there.* Everything I cared about was in that house, too, and I'd managed to keep everyone safe through another crisis. So maybe deadbeat dads weren't my only specialty.

The November twilight was a deep blue, a few brilliant stars beaming through the bare branches of the oak trees. Now who the heck was in the backyard?

At first, I thought it might be Tom. Then I looked closer. A graceful figure in an old fashioned dress tossed a ball to a shadowy bulldog. She laughed silently as the dog shook the ball and trotted back to her. She paused and waved at me as if to signal her approval before she and the bulldog faded into the twilight.

Elizabeth Singer, guardian spirit of 302 Grace.

She was blond, of course.

End